# A Nantucket Promise

## A Nantucket Sunset Series

Katie Winters

# Chapter One

Twenty-Two Years Ago

January wasn't a good time to move to New York City. Quentin's wife, Catherine, laughed about this as she collapsed on their bare mattress, which had been delivered to the new apartment only hours before. Her pregnant belly bulged beneath layers of sweaters, and her face still glowed with a California tan. At this moment, Quentin loved her more than he could even understand.

"But it's going to change everything. I know." Catherine said it before Quentin could, waving one finger back and forth between them.

Quentin rubbed his temples, exhausted after a strenuous day of hauling boxes up to their third-story Brooklyn apartment. The new place cost about as much as their Los Angeles apartment had, but it was half the square footage. Outside, slush lined the streets, and the temperature lulled around thirty-three.

Quentin and Catherine had moved to New York City for Quentin's new job at a top news station. This had come after two years of Quentin's tired attempts to rise in the ranks at the LA station and four years after he'd officially quit acting. The move felt necessary. It meant Quentin was headed toward something.

"So, will I see you on the air tonight?" Catherine smiled and propped her head up with her hand.

Quentin blushed and gestured vaguely at the box labeled "TV." "I don't know who you think you married, but setting up technology like that isn't exactly my thing."

Catherine pouted playfully. "My mother always told me not to date an actor."

"I'm not an actor, baby. I'm a journalist." Quentin paused for a moment, then added, "But I married a much better journalist than me."

"Don't you dare compliment me at a time like this." Catherine gave him a look that read, *don't mess with me.* "I can barely walk, let alone break a story."

Still, it was true. Quentin had met Catherine at a newspaper out west during a high in her career. She'd been on the brink of breaking a huge story about corporate greed at a well-known magazine known for its "altruistic" leanings. Over a round of drinks, Catherine's eyes had spat fire as she'd described her love of journalism, her desire to use words to change the world, and her stories of her mother, who'd been an actress before her untimely death. It had taken Quentin three dates to tell her the truth about his family— that his father was in prison, and he no longer spoke to his three sisters. Catherine had listened intently and known intuitively not to ask questions. They'd married within the year.

New York City wasn't such a difficult move for either of them, though. Catherine's sister had just moved there with her boyfriend, whom Catherine didn't like, and a few of Quentin's friends from his acting days had come to pursue a life in finance. After the birth, Catherine planned to rejoin the world of print journalism, as it was important for her to show their daughter that women could do anything. They could be mothers and businesswomen and excellent cooks and still have time for a drink and a laugh with loved ones.

Perhaps Catherine and Quentin were naive about the future. But wasn't it necessary for young, expecting parents to be naive?

Before he had to leave for his shift at the station, Quentin unpacked several boxes, tried and failed to set up the television, stretched sheets over the mattress, put the pots and pans in the cupboards, and called Catherine's sister to make sure she could come over that night. Catherine was taking a nap in the shadows of the fading afternoon, and Quentin was too anxious to leave her alone at the apartment by herself. He didn't understand the rules of this city yet.

Quentin entered the thirtieth-floor office space at fifteen minutes past four. This was his fifth day on the job, and he'd already made a splash. Makeup artists, costumers, fact-checkers, and other journalists greeted him by name, excited to have him on board. Since his childhood back on Nantucket Island, he'd been thought of like this. Back on the island, everyone had known him as the All-American Copperfield— the eldest son of the prominent Copperfield couple, Bernard and Greta. Because his father's trial hadn't happened until Quentin had been safe in Los Angeles, he'd been able to pretend it hadn't happened at all. Mostly.

Quentin stepped into his office and quickly read over his notes for the night's stories. Quentin was a second-tier anchor, which meant he recorded everything from robberies to murders to fundraising events. So far, this meant he often had to travel somewhere in the city to stand in front of a department store or an apartment block to discuss the matter at-hand while shivering in below-freezing temperatures. Meanwhile, the "top" anchors, Bethany Rodgers and Max Anderson, manned the desk there at the studio, comfortable in their layers of makeup and their expensive suits. Quentin's real goal was that desk. He'd told Catherine over and over again he wanted to be one of the greats. No, he didn't just want to be. He would be.

It was mind over matter. Quentin believed this in his soul.

Quentin was called to the makeup room, where he sat beneath warm lights as a fifty-something-year-old woman with pink eyeshadow applied foundation to his cheeks and complimented his bone structure. Quentin laughed and said, "My wife says compliments like that go to my head." The makeup artist replied, "Your wife sounds like a smart woman. She knows how handsome you are. And she knows that power can be a very dangerous thing."

When his makeup was nearly finished, one of the producers stepped through the door and called his name. Quentin turned quickly, like a dog who heard his food pouring into a bowl. He knew he had to be on his best behavior with his new bosses; he had to show them what he was made of.

The producer's face was strained. He had the look of someone who'd just had several very difficult conversations. "Quentin, it's your first week on the job. I wouldn't ask you to do this if I didn't think you were up for it."

Quentin was always up for a challenge. Bernard Copperfield had called him Quentin "Danger" Copperfield from the ages of four to sixteen until Quentin had privately asked him to stop calling him that in public.

"Whatever it is, I'm your man," Quentin told the producer.

* * *

Minutes later, Quentin was in conversation with Bethany Rodgers, the other nightly news anchor who many called "America's Sweetheart." She was in her mid-thirties with very bright teeth. She had three children and was, therefore, relatable. The viewers had children of their own, too. Theirs played soccer, got into fights, had to do their homework, and left messes around the house, just like Bethany's. Toward the end of every night's broadcast, she usually mentioned them, which led her co-anchor, Max, to laugh and ask questions.

"I told Max not to go to London," Bethany said, her nostrils flared as she regarded Quentin angrily. "It was an idiotic pursuit. He's needed here at the station. America needs him at that desk as many nights as possible. His presence makes Americans feel safe."

Apparently, Max had been stranded in London. Someone had flushed a scarf down the toilet in the airplane, and the airplane had been evacuated. Although Max did have a great deal of money and the backing of the station, he would be almost an hour late. They needed someone to sit in his seat and read the news. They needed someone dominant, confident, and respectable. They needed someone like Quentin.

"I promise that I won't let you down," Quentin told Bethany.

"You'd better not," Bethany returned icily.

Quentin couldn't help but think she was a lot different than her on-air persona. *Was every person on television a lie?* Was he? He made a promise to himself, here and now, to try to remain true to himself. *What you see is what you would get.*

The news was set to begin at eight sharp, just as it had for the previous forty years. Another layer of makeup was applied to Quentin's face, and as the artist worked her magic across his cheekbones and late-twenties' blemishes, Quentin practiced his dictation. Alliteration helped, along with tongue twisters. *"Molly made me mash my M&Ms,"* was a favorite, followed by *"Sally sells seashells by the seashore."* He couldn't remember the last time he'd made a mistake. He had total control over his tongue.

Forty-five minutes before they were set to go on-air, one of the interns hustled into his dressing room. Her eyes were manic. "Excuse me. Mr. Copperfield?"

Quentin was surprised at how fearful the intern looked. Suddenly, because he'd been promoted for the night, his power terrified people. "Yes, what's wrong?"

"Your wife's sister just called." The intern swallowed. "Your wife is in labor. She's at the hospital."

Quentin looked at the intern with wide eyes. He dropped his face into his hands. *Why now?*

"Mr. Copperfield, please. Don't mess up your makeup." The makeup artist had already packed up most of her things and now spoke to him as though he was a child.

Quentin forced his hands away and looked back up at the intern. "On tonight of all nights." He didn't mean to say it. His stress levels were insanely high. He'd been waiting for his big break for years. Now that it was finally here, his daughter had decided to make her appearance, as well. When it rains, it pours.

"Would you like to talk to her?" The intern's eyes watered.

Minutes later, Quentin stood with one of the company phones planted against his ear as Catherine's sister squeaked with terror.

"The baby is coming quickly," she explained. "Catherine's in a lot of pain."

Quentin's heart hammered with dread. Across the studio, Bethany glared at him with her arms across her chest. It was clear she didn't believe in him— not in the slightest.

"How much time do we have?" Quentin hissed.

"The doctor said an hour or two," Catherine's sister replied.

"Can I talk to Catherine?"

"She's in labor, Quentin."

"I know that." Quentin burned with anger and fear. He tried to soften his tone. "Please, put her on. Just for a minute."

There was a rush of movement, followed by the sound of Catherine gasping for breath. Quentin's heart shattered. This was Catherine's greatest time of need. He should have been there.

"Hi, honey." Catherine's voice was jagged and strained. "How's your night going?"

Quentin laughed, surprised at how quick she was with a joke. "I should ask you the same thing."

"You know how much I love surprising you."

"And you always manage to," Quentin said. He smiled into the receiver. After a pause, he added, "I can be there in no time flat if you need me to be. Just say the word."

Catherine puffed air into the phone. "You just started this job, Quentin."

"I know. But you and the baby matter more."

Across the studio, Bethany continued to glower at him. Quentin turned and whispered into the phone.

"But honey, they need me at the desk today."

Catherine's sounds were difficult to decipher. *Did they mean she was in pain? That she was excited?* After another gasp, she said, "Wait. You mean, they want you to read the news? Did Max or Bethany get fired?"

Quentin explained Max had been held up in London. Tonight was a one-time thing.

"But it means you can show them what you're made of."

"You get it." Quentin grimaced. "But I can pass. This is a

big night for us. I want to be with you. I want to be with our baby."

Catherine sounded exhausted, even as she laughed. "I'll try my hardest to keep her in as long as I can. You go read the news, Quentin. It was what you were made to do."

# Chapter Two

Bethany's gaze followed Quentin as he sauntered toward the news desk. As usual, she looked like Barbie's answer to newscasting, with a trim blue pantsuit, poofy blond hair, and bright pink lipstick. Quentin couldn't remember the last story she'd broken on her own and was again reminded of Catherine, who was not a world-renowned name and had never planned to be. Catherine was just a journalist, through and through. She was also hours away from becoming a mother.

"Glad to see you decided to come to the desk. It looked touch and go there for a minute," Bethany said as he sat in Max's usual chair.

Quentin considered telling Bethany about Catherine but held it back. Bethany didn't deserve to know anything about him.

"I'm looking forward to sharing the desk with you tonight," Quentin told her instead.

"We have millions of viewers." Bethany raised both eyebrows. "I'm telling you this not to put the pressure on but instead to remind you of the seriousness of the situation. You're not back in Los Angeles previewing a brand-new taco stand. These are the big leagues."

Quentin locked eyes with her. Behind her icy exterior, he understood something essential. She was terrified of him. Quentin represented all the other confident and successful men she'd fought in her career. No, he hadn't taken her job yet — but that didn't mean he wouldn't eventually try to.

How could he make her understand he wasn't a threat? Then again, didn't he want to be a threat— not just to her, but to everyone in the news world? Didn't he want to be competitive, to rise in the ranks, and to eventually own this very desk, with or without a co-host? The look in her eyes told him the desk would eventually be his. She might not have admitted it, but he could see it.

"How many years have you read the news from this desk?" Quentin asked her, surprising himself.

Bethany feigned a smile. "Really, Quentin. I'm sure you already know the answer to that question."

"I'd love to hear it directly from you."

"Twelve years," Bethany replied, not moving an inch. "And I'm looking forward to twelve more."

Quentin's smile grew. "As are all Americans, I'm sure."

"Bethany? Quentin? We're on in thirty." A young and angular woman on set barked at them as she passed between the cameras.

Behind her, another worker began to count down from thirty. Twenty-nine. Twenty-eight. Twenty-seven. Quentin's stomach tightened into knots. Could he really do this? Across the city, he could feel the pain of Catherine in labor. It felt like a storm over everything else. Didn't he work best under pressure, though? *And wasn't this the greatest pressure of all?*

Ten. Nine. Eight.

Quentin and Bethany stiffened their smiles. The television

in front of them revealed the text they were assigned to read that evening, with quick edits made to account for Max's absence.

Suddenly, the lights shone upon them, hot and steamy. The cameras rolled. Bethany's firm and practiced journalist voice welcomed the viewers that night, saying, "Good evening, and welcome to tonight's edition of Nightly News with Max and Beth. I'm your host, Bethany Rodgers."

"And I'm Quentin Copperfield, standing in for Max," Quentin heard himself say, so confident and sure.

As usual, Bethany set up the first story. "Tonight's top story finds us in Queens, where a gunman held twelve people hostage in a Macy's department store for five hours before the police apprehended him. Afterward, it was discovered that the man's gun was not loaded."

Throughout, Quentin tried to relax into the broadcast. Catherine's face floated in and out of his vision, calling him back to Brooklyn. He was doing this for his family. He was doing this for their future.

After Bethany finished up the unraveling story of the gunman, it was Quentin's turn to read the news.

"Since the holiday season, stock prices have taken a nosedive," he heard himself say, "which has left many in Wall Street scratching their heads."

In the studio, cameramen and camerawomen, sound guys, and light workers regarded him stoically. He felt the importance of what he said as he imagined his face projected across millions of televisions from the Atlantic to the Pacific. Vaguely, he wondered if Greta, Alana, Julia, or Ella watched the nightly news. *What would they think?* Would they even recognize his face after so many years apart?

*Did they show the news in prison?* Quentin had no idea. He didn't like to think of Bernard's living conditions. He didn't like to think of Bernard at all.

The hour rushed by. When the camera cut for the night, the studio workers applauded the evening's work. Bethany draped her soft hand over Quentin's arm, and Quentin nearly jumped. Her eyes were different than they'd been only an hour before. They respected him.

"You were wonderful," she said, sounding hesitant. "Thank you for stepping in."

"It was my pleasure, Mrs. Rodgers," Quentin said. For the first time, he wondered what her maiden name had been. *Did it bother her that her husband's name was a famous name rather than her own?*

Then again, he'd considered dropping his own last name as a way to untether himself from his father. Bernard Copperfield had only been in prison four years; he would be locked up for another twenty-one. Perhaps in that time, the world's interest in Bernard's crimes would completely disintegrate. Perhaps that disintegration had already begun.

"You've got a bright future here." A producer appeared at Quentin's left, smiling eagerly. "You've got that All-American look to you, along with a voice Americans can trust."

Quentin unlatched his microphone from his suit jacket and continued to smile. As he responded, he continued to inch toward the door, drawn like a magnet to his wife's hospital bed. "I do hope I can be what the station needs me to be," he said. "I have a feeling I was led to this role for a reason."

"Between you and me," the producer continued, stepping alongside Quentin as he hustled back to his dressing room, "the station hasn't been pleased with Max's work in quite some time. This London debacle has only added fuel to the fire."

Quentin cocked a single eyebrow. "I hadn't planned to come to the station and rock the boat too much."

"Oh, but you should." The producer's smile was secretive, a mask over something ecstatic. "Life is too short not to rock the boat. Heck, you're good enough, you should be flipping the boat over."

Minutes later, Quentin burst into the back of a cab, still reeling from the night. He asked the cab driver to take him to the hospital in Brooklyn, and then he added, "And step on it," as though this was a silly Hollywood movie and not his real life. The cab drove his best through the slush-filled streets and the bustling darkness. Meanwhile, Quentin sat in the back and stewed in his own excitement for a future he'd always dreamed of. "You can be whatever you want to be," Greta Copperfield had told him before he'd fallen asleep at night. "As long as you're good and kind and open to the possibilities of the universe, you can build whatever life you want."

*Was Greta already a grandmother?* Quentin wasn't sure if any of his siblings had had children of their own yet. He was pretty sure they all had romantic partners. Julia had broken up with her long-time high school boyfriend and moved to Chicago with some guy. Alana was either in New York or Paris, or Timbuktu. He was never sure. That was the life of a model. Then there was Ella, whose indie band had rocketed through the music charts. He was pretty sure she lived in some trendy part of the city as well— but he hadn't yet reached out. Maybe he would if he had time.

A nurse led Quentin to Catherine's room in the labor and delivery ward. Quentin felt frantic; his hands were clammy. When he walked into her room, he found his wife with a red and blotchy face, her hair in a messy ponytail, and her eyes watery with fear. Catherine's sister scowled at him and said, "It's about time." Between gasps, Catherine said, "Don't worry! Don't worry." She then nodded toward the television that hung from the wall and said, "We saw you. We couldn't hear you, but we saw you."

A nurse bustled into the room with a clipboard. She looked

Quentin up and down, perplexed. "You were the young man on the news."

"He was, indeed. My husband, the star." Catherine winced and puffed her cheeks.

"You think that's something? You're about to see something a whole lot greater than that." The nurse gave Quentin a sneaky smile, then proceeded to check how dilated Catherine was. Quentin hurried to the side of Catherine's bed, took her hand, and covered her fingers and palms with kisses. Love for her made him feel swollen.

"I'm so sorry. I should have come right away." Quentin whispered this when both Catherine's sister and the nurse were out of the room.

Catherine shook her head. "You were incredible. I wouldn't have let you miss it for the world."

"This baby is our world," Quentin returned.

Catherine's smile was soon torn apart with pain. Her hand threatened to break the bones in his. "Just stay with us, now. Just promise me you won't go."

"I promise."

Over the next forty-five minutes, Catherine fought valiantly and soon delivered a healthy, screaming seven-pound, six-ounce baby girl. Quentin cut the umbilical cord, then once she was cleaned up, he held the baby in his arms, amazed by this little bundle of joy that he and his wife had created together. It was true what the nurse had said. Her birth had been far greater than being on the news. It had been the most tremendous and magical thing he'd ever witnessed.

And now, as he held her, he felt the crushing weight of real responsibility. Before this, he'd only been Quentin Copperfield, a man with too much ambition and very thick hair. Now, he was a man with a baby. Now, he was a "family man."

When Greta had gotten pregnant with Quentin, she and Bernard had been living in Paris. They'd both had aspirations in the fields of literature, art, music, and academia— but they retreated from Paris to raise Quentin on the quiet and beautiful island of Nantucket. *Had they regretted that move? Maybe.* But Quentin now understood that babies were so wonderful that they outweighed any regret.

Catherine held her daughter afterward. Her eyes glinted with tears. Outside their hospital room was the hustle and bustle of so many other new mothers and brand-new babies and anxious fathers. But behind their closed door was the comfort and beauty of their family of three.

"I can't believe this." Quentin's throat was tight.

Catherine nodded. "It's real."

"She has so much black hair!"

"Like you," Catherine said. Signs of pain slowly drifted off her face, leaving only an exhausted smile. "Do any of the names we picked out fit her?"

Quentin considered the baby's adorable face. Any "adult" name seemed overwhelming for such a little baby. Still, as a person in the world, she deserved one. He ran over the list of names they'd already discussed— Quinn, Brianna, Rhiannon. One night, they'd laughed for hours, coming up with silly names their daughter would hate them for.

Like always, Quentin felt drawn to a single name.

"I still think Scarlet Copperfield is a beautiful and powerful name," Quentin said softly.

"Scarlet." Catherine tilted her head to peer at their daughter's face. "I love the name, too."

"Really?"

*Could it be so simple?* Friends of theirs had fought tooth and nail about their babies' names. Quentin had secretly thought those fights were indicative of bigger issues, but he hadn't dared to dream he and Catherine would be so different.

Catherine nodded and smiled wider. "Scarlet Copperfield, the first child of Quentin and Catherine Copperfield."

"The first of many," Quentin added with a laugh.

Catherine winced. "Let's not talk about any more babies until after I've healed. Or, better yet, when I say so. That was really something."

"Of course. There's no rush." He paused and closed his eyes. Emotion rushed through him. *Was any of this actually real?* When he opened his eyes again, he said, "Thank you for giving me the most incredible gift of my life."

"What a night for Quentin Copperfield," Catherine said.

"Our New York City life has been a whirlwind so far," Quentin agreed. "I can't wait to see what happens next."

# Chapter Three

Present Day

Wherever she went in the city, Scarlet Copperfield saw her father's face. He appeared on billboards, massive television screens, and on magazine covers; there was no escape. For her entire life, Quentin Copperfield had been all anyone could talk about— the household name who had helped the country through some of its darkest hours.

As a child, she'd been very proud to be his daughter. But since her teenage years, something had switched. And now, at twenty-two years old, Scarlet and her father were like strangers.

Certainly, Scarlet hadn't told him what she planned to do that particularly dreary afternoon in January. A few days older than her twenty-second birthday and a senior at New York University, she stood in front of the dean's office to request to take a semester off.

Since Scarlet's freshman year, she'd swapped majors more

times than anyone she knew. She'd started as a journalism major to follow in her parents' footsteps, then had swapped to film, taken a few classes in biology and chemistry, gone away for a semester in Rome to study Latin, switched her major to environmental sciences, and then spent an entire semester partying her way to C-averages (which wasn't like her). Like her parents, she loved to learn— but unlike her parents, she didn't feel particularly drawn in any one direction.

Her lack of focus, on top of the previous months of depression and horror, had made going to school all too difficult to bear.

The dean was a short and muscular man with round glasses and an overeager way of speaking. A dying plant was on the windowsill. Scarlet sat across from him and tried not to think about all the hopes her parents had had for her when she'd initially gotten into NYU.

"Hello, Scarlet. It's good to see you again," the dean greeted. He knew who Quentin Copperfield was. It went without saying.

"Thank you." Scarlet adjusted a jet-black curl behind her ear. "And thank you for meeting me today."

"Of course. I do my best to maintain friendships with the students here at the university," the dean lied. NYU was far too big for him to be "close" with students like that. *Who was he kidding?*

"Right." Scarlet paused. "The thing is, I'm in the middle of a family emergency. I need to drop out of school for a semester."

The dean raised his eyebrows. Probably, the concept of a "family emergency" was great gossip for his lunch hour, especially when that gossip had to do with the Copperfields.

"I'm very sorry to hear that," the dean said. "I'm sure it won't be a problem to withdraw you from your courses. Of course, a refund will not be possible."

"I understand." Scarlet still had a partial scholarship to NYU, although her father still paid for most of her tuition. This was the only thing she allowed him to pay for. Rent, food, and anything else she wanted was all her responsibility. She and her boyfriend, Owen, split the rent of their Brooklyn apartment, which she paid for with a waitressing and bartending gig that kept her up too late most nights.

Like many other twenty-two-year-olds, she was exhausted. Like many other fathers of twenty-two-year-old women, Quentin hated Scarlet's boyfriend with reckless abandon. This, too, was a reason for Scarlet and Quentin's falling out. *"Why can't you just accept that I'm in love? I grew up, Dad. Everyone has to."*

"Do you have an estimate as to when you'd like to return to school?" the dean asked.

Scarlet shrugged like a kid. "Maybe this summer. Maybe in the autumn. I don't know. It really depends on what happens with this family emergency."

The dean's eyes flickered. He was clearly dying to know what the emergency was. Scarlet wouldn't tell him. The dean stood, unbuttoned his corduroy jacket, and stretched out his hand for Scarlet to shake.

"Thank you for your honesty today, Scarlet. I look forward to seeing you back on campus soon. Don't hesitate to come in personally."

Back outside, Scarlet stood beneath an overhang and watched a wet snowfall. The students who passed by seemed alien to her. Their expressions were focused, as though they knew exactly where they were headed in the next five years. Why had that never been clear to Scarlet?

Now, there was the issue of her mother. Her breast cancer had rattled Scarlet's already-uncertain existence. With her mother in and out of chemo treatments, her mother's hair raining across the bathroom floor, and her younger siblings panicking and weeping, how could Scarlet make a decision about her future?

It was only noon, which made it nine in LA. The phone rang across the continent and brought Owen's voice to Scarlet's ear. It was open and deep and powerful, and it reminded Scarlet of gravity and kept her on the ground.

"Hi, bunny. How are you?"

"I just had my meeting with the dean."

"How did that go?"

"Oh, fine. I could tell he was really interested in my 'family emergency.' His brain was working overtime."

"Ah, yes. The shadow of Quentin Copperfield," Owen said.

"That's right. I can never escape it." Scarlet's heart ballooned. It was wonderful to feel that someone "got" her. "How's it going out in LA?"

"Really good," Owen told her. "I'm on set now. We just finished rehearsing a really important scene. I'm getting a lot out of the actors, which is amazing. Everyone came to prove themselves."

"That's incredible, Owen. Really. And how does it feel to be in LA? Still think we should move out there soon?"

"It's so sunny and warm, bunny. I had a green drink for breakfast and felt all my New York City toxins coming out of my pores."

"Ew," Scarlet teased him.

Owen laughed. "I miss you. But I'll be home soon."

"Miss you and love you, too."

Scarlet walked the city streets, lost in the chaos of her head and dreaming about Owen and the life they would build together. She'd met him at an NYU party two years ago when she'd been twenty, and he'd been twenty-four. At the time, he'd been an up-and-coming filmmaker and had recently worked with Werner Herzog on a project in South Africa.

Although she'd begged him to, he'd refused to do a Werner Herzog accent, saying that he wanted to "respect" the great master. After three more tequila shots, he'd broken down and made the worst Herzog impression Scarlet had ever heard. She'd fallen in love with him at that moment when he'd revealed the depths of his flaws. They'd been inseparable ever since.

Scarlet had introduced Owen to her parents that summer. They'd met at a barbecue place on the Upper West Side, where a rack of ribs had cost fifty-five dollars. Owen had talked about a documentary he'd worked on about "real" barbecue in the south, where a rack of ribs had cost about six dollars and had come with a massive side of macaroni and cheese. Quentin hadn't liked that conversation; he'd thought Owen was poking fun at Quentin's money and all his hard work. Since then, ever since Quentin and Owen had crossed pasts, it had been tense. Scarlet's mother had told Scarlet not to worry about Quentin's moods. "Your daddy just doesn't want you to grow up."

Scarlet's parents had moved into their Upper West Side apartment when Scarlet was four. Quentin had officially been named head anchor of the nightly news, booting both Bethany Rodgers and Max Anderson from the desk. The promotion required a completely different lifestyle. Quentin Copperfield had needed to be "seen." The Brooklyn apartment hadn't cut it anymore.

By then, of course, Ivy had been born. James came two years later. Together, the family of five had lived in a luxurious apartment on the Upper West Side as Quentin's name rose in prominence. "Your daddy was always meant to be somebody," their mother had always said. Scarlet had always wondered if Catherine was jealous of Quentin.

Before her diagnosis, Catherine had still worked as a freelance journalist. Unfortunately, her husband's fame made it much more difficult for her to dig for interesting stories. She couldn't always get her hands dirty. She had to "think of the bigger picture."

When Scarlet entered the apartment building, Ivy and James were in the lobby, sharing a package of Reese's cups. Ivy could have been Scarlet's twin, with long, raven hair and sharp cheekbones, while James took after Catherine's side of the family and had rounder features and happier smiles. Scarlet loved them both to pieces.

"My babies!" Scarlet hustled forward and wrapped her arms around them.

Ivy rolled her eyes and stepped back as James grinned and waved the empty Reese's package in the air. "Oops."

"I get it. Why would you share with your older sister?" Scarlet teased them and stepped toward the elevator.

"Aren't you supposed to be in school?" Ivy asked as they entered the elevator.

"I got out early," Scarlet lied. "How was school for you guys today?"

"Annoying," James said.

"I have senior-itis," Ivy explained with a shrug. "My friends and I all do. Four more months of school seems like prison."

"Just wait till you're in college," Scarlet warned. "Everything gets a whole lot harder."

Ivy had decided to go to NYU, as well, which both pleased and terrified Scarlet. NYU was not for the faint of heart. Scarlet prayed her sister wouldn't get into as much trouble as she had.

"Finally, I'll get to move into the big bedroom," James said. "I've been waiting for sixteen years!"

"We talked about this. You can't have it yet. What if I need it when I come back to visit?" Ivy asked.

The elevator dinged and opened directly into their apartment, which took up the entire floor. The maid had come recently; shoes were lined neatly near the welcome mat, and the hardwood floors glistened. From the elevator, there was no sign of their mother's cancer. It could have been any other year.

"Mom has chemo today at four-thirty," Scarlet explained, her voice authoritative. "So, when we get back, I need the house to be as quiet as possible."

Ivy and James nodded, both of them sullen. They headed to their bedrooms and closed the doors behind them, leaving Scarlet to check on their mother. According to the schedule, Quentin had left for work about a half-hour before. Soon, Scarlet would ready her mother and take her downstairs, where Quentin's driver would pick them up and take them to the clinic. After chemo, the driver would return them to the apartment, where Scarlet would wait up until Quentin's return.

This was the family schedule that she and Quentin had arranged. It allowed them to spend very little time together and ensured Catherine hardly spent any time alone. Catherine was their top priority.

Catherine was awake and perched on the side of the bed. She had a magenta scarf wrapped around her bald head and a long sweater dress over her slender frame. Her eyes were hollowed out, but her smile was serene and easy.

"There's my girl," Catherine said, raising her arms to hug Scarlet.

Scarlet allowed herself to be hugged. She hated how weak and thin her mother felt in her arms. She hated cancer with all her heart.

On the way to chemo, Catherine and Scarlet spoke gently in the back seat. Scarlet liked to get as much conversation with her mother out of the way before chemo, as Catherine was normally too tired after her treatment to say much of anything.

"How is Owen's project?" Catherine asked.

"It sounds like it's going really well," Scarlet explained. "I know he's always happiest when he's working."

"That's wonderful, honey. I know you're proud of him. I hope they pay him well," Catherine said.

Scarlet wanted to remind her mother that she and Owen paid their rent on time every single month without Quentin's help. But this wasn't the time for such a conversation.

"I wish Dad could see how talented he is," Scarlet said instead.

Catherine nodded. "He'll understand someday. You have to give him time."

Scarlet bristled. "I met Owen two years ago. Isn't that enough time?"

"Your father is under tremendous pressure," Catherine reminded Scarlet. "He's missed several nights at the newscaster desk since this silly cancer diagnosis."

"The news isn't everything," Scarlet scoffed.

"I know that. Your father knows that."

"Does he?"

Catherine flashed Scarlet a dangerous look. "Since my diagnosis, he's gone out of his way for me in so many ways."

Scarlet bowed her head. She knew this. In fact, she'd been surprised at how easily Quentin had dropped the station in pursuit of her mother's health.

"He could lose his job," Catherine continued. "After all he's given to the station, they could take everything away from him."

Scarlet wanted to say she didn't care. Still, something held her back. Perhaps she loved her father too much to wish him any real ill will. Perhaps, just like Quentin, she had no idea who Quentin Copperfield would be without the nightly news.

# Chapter Four

Quentin used to live to be behind a camera. The lights blaring and the cameras pointed at him were thrilling; even his own voice, booming through the room, had reminded him of the depths of his journalistic mission. As everyone across America had tuned in to listen to what he had to say, he'd grown to think of himself as a God. Certainly, nothing bad could ever happen to a God.

Things were different now. Since Catherine's diagnosis, he'd felt at a distance from the rest of the world. His thoughts often drifted, which made it difficult for him to read the teleprompter. He no longer cared about the ratings of each nightly news segment. He lived for the moment when he could remove his microphone, take off his thick suit jacket, and head home to care for Catherine.

That night, the cameras cut at nine o'clock sharp. Quentin immediately lost his powerful facade. He slumped over in the news chair and listened as the workers in the studio bustled around him, preparing for the next taped segment. When one of the producers called his name, Quentin slowly removed his microphone and limped off-screen to shake his hand.

"Great show, as always," the producer said. His eyes told a different story. They looked like all the other eyes in the studio, foggy with doubt about Quentin's new lack of talent. Where was the Quentin Copperfield they'd all known and loved? What had happened to him?

Quentin changed into a pair of jeans and a black long-sleeved shirt. In the mirror of his dressing room, his eyes were hollow. For the first time in hours, he checked his phone to find several messages from Scarlet, who explained they'd finished chemo and were now back at home. She'd made a pot of chili, which he could have if he wanted. Quentin's heart was battered and bruised. Scarlet loved him just as he loved her. But they didn't like each other right now. That was clear.

As Quentin packed up his things for the night, his sister, Alana, called him. Alana was the closest to Quentin in age, which meant they'd been closer as kids. She got away with contacting him a lot more than his other two sisters.

"Hey." Quentin sounded stiff.

"Hi. Is this a bad time?"

"I just got off the air."

"I know. I was watching with Mom and Julia." Alana sounded hesitant. "How are you holding up?"

It was clear she'd felt she needed to reach out to him. Perhaps he'd looked out of his mind on the news. Great.

"I'm fine. Really." He paused. "Scarlet took Catherine to chemo today. I'm about to head home to see them."

"Oh, Quentin." Alana's voice quivered. "I'm just so sorry this is happening."

Quentin was, too. He was so sorry. He was sorry that he wasn't sure how to live in the real world anymore. Last December, his father and his sister, Julia, had come to New York City and basically demanded to see him, as they'd suspected something was up. When Quentin had finally broken down and told them about Catherine's cancer, Bernard had suggested Quentin move his family to Nantucket, where the Copperfields could help him deal with the emotional toll of Catherine's cancer. This had infuriated Quentin. Why would he uproot his entire family? What did Bernard think he could do to help? *Hadn't Bernard been nothing but a nuisance for nearly twenty-six years?*

Okay, it was true Bernard wasn't guilty of the crimes he'd been in prison for. But it was also true that his prison sentence had broken up Quentin's family, thus destroying his emotional base. Catherine had been the first person he'd met who'd made him feel whole again.

If he lost Catherine to this cancer, there would be no point to life anymore.

"Have you given any thought to coming to Nantucket?" Alana asked.

Quentin switched immediately from sorrow to annoyance. "The move back to Nantucket worked for you, Julia, and Ella," he said simply. "But I can't just move to that little island. What would I do? Where would my career go?"

Alana sighed. "Careers aren't everything, Q."

This was easy for Alana to say. She'd married a horrific, career-driven artist who'd subsequently ruined her life. Now, she'd gotten back together with her high school boyfriend, taught acting classes at The Copperfield House, and cooked every night with their mother. Happiness was suddenly easy for her. She wasn't America's number-one news source. She wasn't Quentin.

Quentin's driver picked him up outside the office. In the backseat, the warm lights from the city washed over him. Although Quentin had once enjoyed a wonderful friendship with his driver, he was now too lost in his head to speak.

Alana's words, "Careers aren't everything," swirled in his

mind. For some reason, all he could feel was regret. Since he'd moved Catherine to New York City, he'd worked tirelessly to get to the top of the nightly news field. He'd championed over Bethany and Max; the desk had become his. But in the years since, it was impossible to calculate how much time he'd lost with his family. He'd missed ballet recitals. He'd missed orchestra competitions. He'd missed basketball scrimmages, wedding anniversaries, birthday parties, trips to the Hamptons, barbecues, and even some bigger family vacations, which he'd had to drop out of at the last minute. Catherine had always been pretty good about understanding. *"I knew I married a driven man."* Then again, why hadn't he considered how little time he had with his children in the first place? Why hadn't he considered that Scarlet would one day grow up, move out, and move in with some slimy filmmaker named Owen?

Why hadn't he considered that one day, Catherine might die?

* * *

The apartment was warm and inviting, filled with the savory smells of spicy chili and toasted garlic bread. Quentin removed his shoes, coat, and hat and greeted Ivy and James, who sat in their pajamas in the living room and stared at their phones as the television played a basketball game. Ivy and James turned to smile at him. "Scar made chili," Ivy explained. "She's with Mom right now."

Quentin thanked her. "How was your day?"

James and Ivy exchanged glances. At sixteen and eighteen, they were deep in the chaos of high school and teenage hormones. Quentin was glad they had each other.

"It was fine," James said. "How was the show?"

"Fine." Quentin hated the word "fine." Was he capable of having a human conversation with his children? Could he say that, actually, today was hot garbage, and tomorrow probably would be, too? He wasn't sure.

In the back of the house was the sound of Catherine getting sick. Quentin's stomach twisted with sorrow. The chemo always did this. He should have been used to it by now. Then again, it wasn't necessarily something he wanted to get used to.

Quentin entered the bedroom he shared with Catherine. The bathroom door was cracked, and inside, Scarlet spoke gently to Catherine.

"It's okay, Mom. It's okay. Do you think you can make it back to bed?"

Catherine responded, but Quentin couldn't make out what she said. A moment later, shadows filled the bathroom doorway, and Catherine finally appeared, her head slumped.

"Oh. Quentin." Catherine tried a smile. "I didn't hear you come in."

Scarlet held Catherine's arm gently as they walked back to bed. As usual, Quentin was struck by the tenderness Scarlet showed her mother. She was a caretaker with the skill and kindness of a much older woman.

Quentin leaped forward to guide Catherine the rest of the way to bed. "How are you, darling?" He helped her sit on the edge of the bed and then sat beside her, cupping her hand.

The image was too powerful for Scarlet, so she dropped her gaze.

"We had quite a day," Catherine said. "But Scarlet has been a trooper. I can't thank her enough for helping me."

Quentin nodded and stared at Scarlet, willing her to lift her eyes. "She is a tremendous help."

Scarlet raised her hand, waved it, and said, "I'm going to grab a bowl of chili." She then disappeared into the hallway.

Quentin kissed Catherine on the cheek, on the ear, and on the top of her forehead, where her hair had once come in. Cancer was a monster. Why had it chosen his beautiful bride?

"I love you, Catherine," Quentin told her gently as she lay back on the pillow.

"I know you do." Catherine smiled sheepishly. "I guess I love you, too."

"You guess?"

Catherine stuck out her tongue playfully. "I'm going to fall asleep in no time flat. Why don't you go out and hang with your daughter?"

"I don't think she wants anything to do with me."

"She's just as stubborn as you are. Like father, like daughter."

When Catherine drifted to sleep, Quentin returned to the living room, where Scarlet hovered above the couch, ate her chili, and chatted with Ivy and James. Typical of younger children, Ivy and James were always pleased when Scarlet was around. They viewed her as the most intelligent person in the world. In truth, Scarlet was terribly smart— she just had no idea where to direct those smarts. She'd even gotten C-averages one semester. Quentin wasn't proud of what he'd said to her because of it.

Quentin poured himself a bowl of chili and sat at the island, listening to the delightful pattern of his children's conversation. *Had Bernard once listened to the Copperfield children with the same amount of love and affection?*

When there was a lull in the conversation, Quentin said, "This chili is really good, Scar. Thank you."

Scarlet turned and arched her eyebrow. "Um. Thanks."

"What did you put in it?"

"Chili beans. Ground beef. Peppers. You know. Chili ingredients." She was sassy as ever.

Quentin searched his mind for a way to tell her how much he missed her. "Wow. I had no idea you were such a good cook."

"I've lived on my own for a few years," Scarlet pointed out. "Owen and I cook all the time."

Quentin sniffed. Gosh, he hated that Owen kid. "Owen's lucky to have a cook like you in the house."

"We both cook, Dad. We don't subscribe to traditional gender roles."

"I know that." Quentin realized he'd done something wrong. All the color drained from Scarlet's cheeks. He could feel her hostility from across the room. "I'm just saying, I'm sure Owen appreciates how talented you are."

"Right. Because you think he's so untalented. Is that it?"

Quentin's anger rose steadily. Yes, he thought Owen was an imbecile. He'd googled one of Owen's film projects— a music video for a metal band, and he'd thought it was very amateur for someone who'd supposedly been making films for over five years. Quentin was "in the business." He knew what he was talking about. Didn't he?

"I didn't say Owen was untalented," Quentin said instead.

"Not this time." Scarlet hustled around the island and scrubbed her bowl in the sink. After a dramatic pause, she said, "I'll come back tomorrow, same time. Does that work for you?"

Quentin nodded and stared at the floor. "Thanks for coming."

"Someone has to be here to help," Scarlet shot back. She then headed for her coat and boots, shoving them on angrily.

Quentin locked eyes with Scarlet. He wanted to tell her how much he loved her. He wanted to tell her that she didn't have to do this whole "being twenty-two and lost" thing on her own. But, just as Catherine had said, he was stubborn, the same as she was. He allowed Scarlet to turn on her heel and enter the elevator, calling back a "goodnight" to her brother and sister.

When Scarlet was gone, Ivy turned to look at her father. "I wish she would move home, too, Dad."

Quentin nearly burst into tears.

# Chapter Five

Scarlet took the subway back to Brooklyn. On the train, she texted Owen furiously about how angry she was with her father. She wrote that he made no effort to understand her and that he was responsible for the rift that continued to widen. Of course, she didn't text Owen what was truly weighing on her: that her mother was terribly sick, that she was worried about her siblings, and that she'd just made the terrifying decision to drop out of school. It had been a day for the books.

It was nearly eleven at night by the time Scarlet stepped off the subway. Brooklyn was night to the Upper West Side's day, a chaotic and trendy series of neighborhoods that had gentrified too quickly and resulted in third-wave coffee shops, cocktail bars, restaurants that sold only bowls with ingredients she couldn't pronounce the names of, and expensive Mexican places that called themselves "holes in the wall." To this, Owen always joked, "Isn't Mexican food just beans and rice? Why is this burrito eighteen dollars?"

Owen hadn't texted Scarlet back. This wasn't a surprise. It

was only eight in LA, which meant he was probably finishing up work, socializing with his colleagues, and planning for the next day. Scarlet imagined him with a black baseball hat, pointing at an image on the screen as he instructed a cinematographer on how best to attack the next day's scene. Gosh, she loved him. She adored how creative his mind was and how he'd managed to build an entire career based on that creativity. Maybe one day, she'd figure out how to do that, as well.

In fact, to Scarlet, marrying Owen Wellesley wasn't such an insane proposition. Yes, she was young. Owen was young, too. But in her mind, Owen's career was already on the fast track to greatness. If she latched herself to his rocket, she would surely find herself on the way to the top. Perhaps at that top, she would become a renowned artist, a musician, or a writer, like her mother. Perhaps with Owen's guidance, she would finally find her own wings.

The apartment Scarlet and Owen shared was located on the second floor of an up-and-coming apartment building, which was filled with artists who were similarly up-and-coming. Scarlet loved the creative spirit in the building; it was the feeling that anything could happen at any time. Unlike most Manhattan apartments, however, theirs didn't have a doorman, which had initially freaked Scarlet out. Could she trust the "wild" streets of Brooklyn?

Since their move-in, however, they'd had no troubles at all, so much so that Scarlet had begun to think of the apartment as "home," much more than the apartment she'd grown up in. This was a remarkable thing. She was really growing up.

Scarlet took the stairs to the second floor. Once there, she went into autopilot, turning her key in the door and walking into the apartment. It was only when she turned on the lights that she realized something was dreadfully wrong.

Everything was gone.

Scarlet screamed, but the scream was hardly more than a

rasp. She smacked her hand over her lips as her eyes scanned the living room, where the enormous flat-screen television had once hung on the wall. It was gone, as were the expensive decorations her mother had given her. Scarlet's heart slammed against her ribcage.

Directly next to the living room was the kitchen. Scarlet turned on the lights to show a mostly intact room. Only the expensive china she'd had in the decorative cabinet was gone.

"Oh my God. Oh my God." Scarlet muttered to herself as tears rolled down her cheek. She fumbled for her phone and initially pulled up her father's phone number. If she called him, he would be there in no time flat. He would pull strings at the police station. He would make all this terror go away.

But then again, she wanted nothing to do with her father. Why would she call him when times got rough? Wasn't she an adult? Couldn't she handle this on her own?

Instead, Scarlet backed into the hallway, closed the door to her apartment, and called Owen. Owen answered on the third ring.

"Hello, darling. How's your evening?"

Scarlet hardly recognized her voice. "Owen. We've been robbed!"

"What? What are you talking about?" Owen's tone shifted from honey to ice.

"I just got home," Scarlet stuttered, "and the TV is gone. The nice decorations from my mother are gone. The china is gone." She swallowed. "I haven't gone into the bedroom or the office. I'm too scared, Owen."

A part of her wanted to scream, *"why aren't you here with me?"*

"Don't go back in there, baby," Owen told her firmly. "It's too dangerous. Whoever took the stuff could still be back there, going through more things."

"Why did they do this to us, Owen?" Scarlet demanded, sounding confused. "Why would they do this?"

"This happens, Scar," Owen told her. "The best thing about it is you weren't home. Okay? You're safe. That's all that matters. Now, promise me this. You'll go across the hallway, knock on the door, and get Brad. Brad should be home tonight, right?"

"Brad's always home." Brad was an unemployed man with an online gambling addiction who hardly left his apartment.

"Right. So, go knock on his door. Ask him to stand with you until the police arrive."

"Okay." Scarlet turned to stare at Brad's door. She did not want to knock on it at all. Still, she trusted Brad. He was kind, with large hands and soft eyes. He could beat up an intruder if he wanted to.

"Call me after the police get there," Owen said.

"Okay." Scarlet sniffed. "I love you."

"I love you, too."

Brad waited with Scarlet outside the apartment door for the ten minutes it took the police to arrive. Brad was eager to go into the apartment himself to "investigate," but Scarlet held him back. The last thing she wanted was for Brad to get injured.

When the police came, they searched through the apartment and gave it the all-clear. Scarlet was relieved and followed them toward the bedroom she shared with Owen, where she discovered all her jewelry missing. Tears welled in her eyes. Many of those pieces had been birthday and graduation gifts; they represented memories she could never get back. Even the locket her mother had given her was gone. This was particularly devastating, as it had held a photo of her mother and one of Scarlet as a little girl.

As the police made a report, Scarlet called Owen back to

tell him the thieves had taken upwards of twenty-five thousand dollars in goods. That was just her initial estimate.

"Oh, baby." Owen sighed, clearly at a loss.

"Do you think they targeted me?" Scarlet demanded. "Do you think they knew I would have so many expensive things because of my father?"

"I don't know. It's possible. Then again, people get robbed in this city for all sorts of random reasons. Not everything comes back to your father."

Owen urged Scarlet to contact her girlfriend, Alyssa, for emotional support. "You shouldn't be alone tonight. I don't want you to be in that apartment until I get back." He then promised he would be there by the end of the week to help her sort through the logistics of being robbed.

After their call, Scarlet called Alyssa, praying she was around. Alyssa was something of a wild card. For years, the girls had grown up together in Manhattan, both daughters of very rich and semi-famous men. Devastatingly, Alyssa's father cheated on her mother with her mother's best friend and then died of a heart attack not long after. Since then, Scarlet had done her best to help Alyssa pick up the pieces of her life again. Of course, Alyssa had needed space from the city— and she now spent many weeks at a time on Martha's Vineyard at her grandmother's beachside home.

Scarlet's heart leaped into her throat with relief when Alyssa answered.

"Babe! Are you out?" Alyssa asked.

"Alyssa. I got robbed," Scarlet cried.

"What? I can't hear you! The bar is really loud."

Quickly, Scarlet packed a bag of clothing (noting that some of her more expensive designer outfits were missing) and hurried off to meet Alyssa. It was better to explain what had happened in person.

Alyssa sat at the bar with two other of Scarlet's girlfriends,

Renée and Bree. They greeted her with joyous shrieks and hugged her. Scarlet collapsed on the stool beside Alyssa, her eyes buggy.

"What the heck happened to you?" Alyssa asked, her head tilted. "You look like you just saw a ghost."

"I got robbed," Scarlet said again. "They took everything of value."

Alyssa's jaw dropped, as did Bree's and Renée's.

"Oh my gosh. Scarlet!" Alyssa grabbed Scarlet's wrist and pulled her into another hug. "Tell us everything that happened."

Scarlet told the story as best as she could. She explained she'd left her parents' house, taken the subway to Brooklyn, and walked into the apartment to find the television gone. All three girls told her it was clearly a nightmare situation. They agreed they were so glad she was okay.

"And Owen's coming back?" Alyssa asked.

Scarlet nodded. "Yeah. He's going to wrap everything up as quickly as he can."

"Dang. Such terrible timing!" Alyssa said.

"I wonder if they knew Owen was gone?" Scarlet asked. "I mean, don't thieves stake places out?"

Bree and Renée nodded. Renée had listened to a podcast about famous robberies. Bree said she'd been meaning to listen to that podcast, which didn't help at all.

"Anyway, I need somewhere to stay," Scarlet told Alyssa.

"Of course! You can stay with my sister and I," she explained. "Maggie lives just around the corner. Tomorrow morning, just wake up whenever you want and help yourself in the kitchen. That's what I do."

Scarlet smiled, swimming in even more relief. "I can't thank you enough."

"Oh, and you shouldn't go to class tomorrow," Alyssa urged. "You need to take care of yourself right now. That means mental health first. Especially with what's going on with your mom."

"I dropped out of school today, actually."

Alyssa was very good about not making a big deal about enormous changes. She'd been through too much to be dramatic.

"It sounds like dropping out was the right choice," she said. "As I said, mental health comes first. You can go back to college whenever you want to. It'll always be there waiting for you."

# Chapter Six

A gray smog settled over New York City. Days passed without the sun, and schedules were laid out unceremoniously. Quentin found himself pulled from the news station back home to care for Catherine on an endless rotation. Since his brief spat with Scarlet the previous week, she'd kept her distance, usually leaving the apartment about five minutes before his arrival. This only exacerbated his anxiety. It told him just how far away his dreams of having a perfect and loving family were. It told him just how wrong he was.

Catherine was in the living room with Ivy. Both of them were in their pajamas, watching television. Ivy nibbled on popcorn. A seat on the sofa to Catherine's left had clearly belonged to Scarlet before her spontaneous departure to get out of her father's way.

"How are my girls doing?" Quentin kissed the top of their heads.

"We're doing just fine." Catherine turned her tired head to smile up at him. Ivy lifted the bowl of popcorn so he could take a handful. In the old days, he would have avoided the salt like the plague, as it caused his face to bloat. These days, he didn't care at all.

Quentin turned into the kitchen to pour himself a mug of tea and grab something to eat. On the couch, Ivy continued to tell her mother a story, something about high school and boys. For not the first time, Quentin questioned what would happen if Catherine died. *Who would Ivy tell those stories to?* Certainly, she wouldn't share them with him.

Exhausted, Quentin poured himself a bowl of James's cereal and added a touch of almond milk, which Scarlet had announced was healthier. He remained standing at the kitchen island and crunched through the cereal, knowing the food wouldn't help his hunger at all. Then again, nothing would.

The kitchen island was where things were dropped off to be picked up later. That was where the mail was deposited, where textbooks waited for the next day's classes. And there, to the left of a Calculus textbook, sat a typed letter addressed to Quentin and Catherine Copperfield. Quentin picked it up.

The letter was from James's advisor. It explained that James was falling behind in several classes, that he'd skipped several the previous week, and that if he didn't get his grades up, he would lose his stance in the National Honor Society, which would subsequently diminish his chances of getting into good schools and honing the career of his dreams. James was only sixteen. It seemed unlikely that anything he did now would affect him at twenty-seven or thirty-one. Then again, the world was much different than it had been in the nineties when Quentin had graduated.

"Where's James?" Quentin asked.

"He's in his room," Ivy said.

"Thanks." Quentin paused and racked his brain for something else to say— something that would remind both Ivy and Catherine how much he loved them. But they were lost in their own conversation. Catherine spoke as though she wasn't currently undergoing the most heinous treatment in the world. Quentin didn't want to bring her down. Not then.

Quentin hovered outside of James's bedroom like a lost puppy. Inside, music played from James's portable speaker. *Was it Slipknot? Nirvana?* Quentin hadn't heard music like it in years. Finally, he got up the nerve to knock, and the music cut out just before James opened the door. His eyes widened with surprise. It wasn't every day that Quentin Copperfield asked for his time.

Maybe that was the problem. Maybe Quentin needed to show just how much he cared about his son and his grades. Scarlet and Ivy had been easy; they'd gotten their homework done and gone to class on time. But the situation had changed since then. Quentin had to remember that.

"Hey, bud." Quentin hated how fake he sounded. "Mind if I come in?"

James shrugged and opened the door wider. Quentin entered the safe haven of his sixteen-year-old son's room, where clothes were strewn across the floor, the bed hadn't been made in many days, and posters of bands Quentin had never heard of adorned the walls. Many years ago, this room had been the Copperfields' last nursery.

With the door closed behind him, Quentin sat at the edge of the bed. James peered at him curiously and ruffled his dark hair. Quentin considered just asking. *What the heck had happened to James's school career?* Then again, wasn't Scarlet currently his number-one enemy, all because he wasn't always so kind with his tone?

"How are you doing?" Quentin asked, feeling unsure of how to start the conversation.

James looked surprised. He shrugged. "Oh. I mean, I'm fine. I'm worried about Mom. But I guess we all are."

Quentin nodded, at a loss. "We're all so worried about

Mom. And I know we're all doing our best to make her comfortable during this horrible time."

James was very still. Quentin was losing steam.

"I just want to make sure we're all doing okay," Quentin continued. "Because we have to take care of ourselves, too. If we don't, we won't be well-equipped to take care of Mom."

James looked very stiff. After a long pause, he muttered, "I already tried to talk to Scarlet."

A rush of panic came over Quentin.

"I mean, I asked her to lighten up on you, because you're obviously under so much stress. But she said she has to handle this her way. I'm sorry." James shrugged again. "Maybe she'll lighten up after the chemotherapy is over."

Quentin struggled against his tears. Here he was, trying to pester his son about his grades, even as his son went out of his way to try to mend their broken family. *What actually mattered in this world?* James seemed to understand better than he did.

"Thank you for doing that," Quentin breathed. "I know I haven't been very good to your sister. I'm going to do everything I can to make it right."

James looked relieved. "That's amazing to hear, Dad. Thank you."

Quentin left James's room after that, defeated. As the door closed, James's speaker roared once more, returning James's room to a haven of teenage angst. Quentin wanted nothing more than to turn around, hug his son, and hide away from the outside world.

* * *

The next afternoon before he left for work, Catherine mentioned Scarlet. This was a rare conversation topic between Catherine and Quentin, especially since they'd fallen into an easy rhythm. The topic of Scarlet wasn't useful to anyone; it only made both of them very sad.

This time, however, as Quentin grabbed his Air Pods and prepared to head downstairs to meet his driver, Catherine said, "Scarlet has been very down lately."

Quentin paused and gave Catherine a sidelong glance. Moodiness in Scarlet wasn't such a strange thing. *How was this different?*

"What do you mean?"

"I don't know. She's been very quiet. When I look at her, her eyes seem very far away, like she's thinking about something very intently. Something she can't share with me."

Quentin paused. "Do you think she and Owen broke up?"

Catherine flashed him a dark look. "Don't, Quentin."

"All right. All right." Quentin lifted his hands in defeat. "I know. I'm the bad guy for thinking that talentless guy isn't good enough for our amazing, intelligent, and beautiful daughter."

"You're not the bad guy," Catherine said. "You just have a habit of making things more difficult than they have to be. Maybe it's the journalist in you."

"I see you're examining me like the journalist you are," Quentin reminded her. "You're always two or three steps ahead of me."

Quentin kissed Catherine goodbye and rushed downstairs and into the car. There, he listened to his Air Pods too loud to pump himself up for the night ahead. There had been a devastating accident in Malibu, which would certainly be the top story, followed by an incident at the NBA that was sure to require coverage. Every few minutes, he was reminded of Catherine's worry about Scarlet, but those thoughts did nothing but rile him up. Whatever was wrong, she wanted to handle it herself. He knew she wanted her life to be private, and he had to respect that.

To him, it would never feel okay. But in order for Quentin to perform the news that night, he had to pretend it was.

Just like always, Quentin entered the chaos of the nightly news studio and greeted everyone by name. He high-fived makeup artists, spoke with PAs, and said hello to interns. In every respect, he imitated the "prosperous Quentin Copperfield" he'd once been. He was king.

In the hallway, on the way to his dressing room, one of the PAs stood in front of a handsome dark-haired man with broad shoulders and piercing eyes. He was the epitome of what America wanted at the news desk. As Quentin neared him, the man lifted his gaze to lock eyes with Quentin. *Who was he?*

"Quentin." The man said his name and smiled a split-second too late. He stretched out his hand to shake Quentin's. "It's wonderful to finally meet you. My name is Jackson Crawford."

Quentin's eyes became slits. *Jackson Crawford? Why was the name so familiar?*

"Hi, Jackson." There was confusion behind his voice. "I'm assuming we've run into each other before. Maybe at a news function or one of those terrible awards parties?"

Jackson laughed. "I did spot you across the room once. But no. Actually, I'm your brother-in-law. Well, ex-brother-in-law. Julia and I signed the papers."

Quentin's jaw dropped. *Of course!* The man before him was Julia's ex-husband, the guy who'd dragged Julia to Chicago and subsequently left her to follow some heinous career path in China. He'd heard through Alana that Jackson was back. *But why here?* Why at Quentin's station?

"I know. It's terrible we were never allowed to interact as brothers-in-law," Jackson continued. "I would have loved to hang out at family barbecues and Christmases. Then again, I know the Copperfield clan isn't the most typical of families."

Quentin's stomach burned with acid and resentment. *Who*

*did this guy think he was? What did he know about the Copperfields?* Then again, he'd been married to Julia for more than twenty years— a lifetime, in some respects.

"Quentin. Hey." One of the head producers passed him in the hallway and gestured for his office. "Can I speak to you for a moment?"

"Good to meet you," Quentin said to Jackson, grateful to step away. The way Jackson looked at him was ominous and predatory. Had he looked at Julia like this before he'd set out to ruin her life and destroy their family?

Then again, if Jackson hadn't divorced Julia, Julia would have never returned to The Copperfield House. The Copperfield children would never have discovered their father's innocence. So much good wouldn't have happened.

But that didn't mean Quentin was ever going to like Jackson Crawford.

"You'll never believe this," Quentin explained as he stepped into the producer's office. "That terrible man back there is my sister's ex-husband."

The producer's eyes were dull. "Oh. That's interesting, isn't it? I always forget you have siblings. I've always taken you for an only child."

Quentin recognized the insult. He was suddenly aware of the closed door behind him. He felt like a trapped animal.

"Quentin, I wanted to take a moment to thank you for the tremendous work you've done for us over the years."

Quentin's nostrils flared.

"And remind you that here at the station, we're a family. We really are. And you've been our guiding light for seventeen years! We've never looked back from that decision."

"Well, you weren't even here for that decision," Quentin pointed out. "You were, what? In high school?"

The producer was unfazed. He looked like a principal dealing with an unruly student. "In any case, as of late, we've noticed a real downturn in ratings. At first, we thought it was nothing to worry about. Things come in waves, as you know. But the trend has been steady and sure for several months now, which has led us to seek out change."

There was a violent ringing in Quentin's ears. "My wife has had cancer for months. It has taken everything within me to keep it together for this station."

"I am very sorry to hear about your wife. You really should have mentioned this to the station sooner."

Quentin bristled. Why should he explain the innermost terrors of his soul to the station that had already stolen so much of his time and energy?

"We aren't asking for you to step down," the producer continued. "It's more of a leave of absence so that you can get your head on straight. It'll be good for all of us to take a break. Seventeen years is a very long time."

Quentin was at a loss for words. The producer gathered a stack of papers on his desk and began to talk about the Knicks. Quentin wanted to punch the wall.

"And Jackson Crawford? He's filling in for me tonight?"

The producer shrugged. "We're going to see how he does."

Quentin bolted out of the producer's office, overwhelmed with rage. Everyone in the halls gave him strange looks, as though they already knew he'd been replaced. He took a right turn, then a violent left, before he stumbled back into the ecosystem of Jackson Crawford.

There he was. He lifted his powerful chin to give Quentin a smile. And before Quentin knew what he'd done, he stormed up to Jackson, raised a finger to his chest, and blared, "How dare you treat my sister that way."

He was suddenly eager for a fight.

"I'm sorry. I don't think this is entirely office-appropriate," Jackson said.

"No. This is the time and the place, you idiot. You dragged

my sister to Chicago, built a life with her, and then abandoned her for some crazy job in Beijing? Are you out of your mind? You know, your children hate you. They can't stand to hear your name, let alone text you back. They told me so themselves last time I was on Nantucket. Poor Anna. Poor Henry. Poor Rachel."

Jackson twitched at each mention of his children's names. Quentin was momentarily pleased he'd affected him.

"They'll go on to live their lives without you," Quentin continued. "They'll have children you won't be allowed to meet. They'll have careers you won't know anything about. And what will you have? That desk?" Quentin pointed across the studio to the very desk that had been his entire world for seventeen years.

At this, Jackson's lips curved into a horrible smile. "It's so ironic to hear you say that. Isn't it?"

Quentin balked. He hadn't expected Jackson to know enough about him to turn the tables.

"Because from what I've heard, you've given your life to this station. You've missed so much of your family's life. At least I waited till my children were out of the house to go after my dreams." Jackson's tone was icy. "And here I am. A grown man. An empty nester. Here to take away the thing you sacrificed everything for. What do you think about that?"

Quentin felt a wave of anger wash over him. He did everything not to punch Jackson square in the face. Instead, he turned on his heel and fled for the elevator, suddenly unsure about every decision he'd ever made. Perhaps his story was one of a man who'd built a kingdom only to watch it burn to the ground.

# Chapter Seven

Since the robbery, Scarlet had lived in a state of shock. Owen's return to New York City after the incident had initially calmed her, but when the film project had required him to tie up loose ends in LA, she'd found herself falling apart again. Scarlet knew her mother sensed something was up— she could see the curiosity and fear in Catherine's eyes. But Catherine was too exhausted to pester her for answers, and Scarlet continued to float through her fears, alone and pining for Owen to return for good.

Scarlet had heard through the grapevine that Quentin had lost the news' desk. It had surprised her how devastated she'd felt about it. Her father, without the desk? Her father, taken off the nightly news? *Who would guide America? Who would say what was right and wrong?* Yes, a part of her was still extremely furious with him, with his behavior. But another part of her, a much bigger part, loved him more than the sun, the moon, and the sky. She wanted him to be happy. She wanted him to be whole.

It had been two weeks since the robbery. Since then,

Scarlet had added several more bolts to the door of the apartment. When Alyssa could swing it, she stayed over. However, Scarlet was alone more often than not, sleeping fitfully as she swung from one worry to another.

But that afternoon, Owen planned to return to New York for a longer period of time. Scarlet was over the moon. With Owen back, they could finally figure out how the insurance worked and purchase essential items— like a new television and a few pieces of jewelry. It wasn't like Scarlet could replace the nostalgic pieces that had been taken. Those were gone for good. *But was it too much to ask to feel like a normal person again?* She wanted to get home, flop on the couch, and watch TV. She wanted to feel at home.

More than that, she wanted to find another apartment. The thieves had entered their place, gone through their belongings, and destroyed her sense of safety. The apartment had been tainted. She wanted to start anew.

Because Scarlet had had so many new locks put on the door, it took her a while to open the door to let Owen in. There he stood, all six-foot-two of him, his blond hair cascading past his ears in California locks. Scarlet rushed into his arms and exhaled into his broad chest. "You're back. You're finally back."

Inside, Owen placed his suitcase against the wall and laughed at the elaborate lock system. "That's really something, Scar."

Scarlet tried to chuckle at herself. "It's been scary to be here alone."

Owen laced his fingers through hers and led her to the couch. There, she dropped her head on his lap as he combed through her hair delicately with the tips of his fingers. Silence swelled around them, one taut with emotion. Scarlet was grateful to be with a man she could be quiet with. She was grateful to feel at peace.

"Sometimes I feel like New York is too dangerous," Scarlet said after a while.

"You grew up here," Owen pointed out.

Scarlet nodded. "I know. But I grew up in a bubble in the Upper West Side. What did I know about fear? From an early age, my Dad had a driver who took me anywhere I wanted to go."

"Have you told your dad about the robbery?"

Scarlet turned around to face him with her head still on his lap. "No. I don't want him to know. He'll find a way to blame us, somehow."

"I don't think I've ever been hated so much by anyone. It's incredible." Owen laughed.

"He's just too stubborn to understand how happy I am."

Owen placed his hand across Scarlet's cheek. "I missed you so much, bunny. I couldn't wait to finish the film and get back to you."

Scarlet's eyes welled with tears. She'd missed him so much that she couldn't find the right words to describe it.

A bit later, Owen and Scarlet dressed up for a reunion dinner. Initially, Scarlet struggled with what to wear, as her designer clothing was off in the wide world somewhere, probably being sold on the internet for incorrect prices. But as she slid her dark jeans over her hips and donned a chic turtleneck, she reminded herself of how little she needed designer things. She'd had enough.

Owen and Scarlet walked to a nearby Colombian restaurant, where they ate and drank cocktails and caught one another up on the time they'd missed. Owen described scenes from his film in detail, which excited Scarlet. She loved hearing how his brain worked and was grateful for the intimate welcome into his world. In return, Scarlet explained the status of her mother's chemotherapy. "They'll have a meeting soon to talk about the next steps. Surgery is a possibility. I think that scares my mom a lot."

Owen asked Scarlet how "life after NYU" was going, and Scarlet explained she struggled to make sense of her days now. She'd taken a few extra shifts at the restaurant, which helped with her money flow. And she'd taken to journaling in the morning, with hopes that it would guide her somewhere.

"I wish I was like you," Scarlet said. "You were born knowing you wanted to be a filmmaker. I was born with no direction."

The waitress arrived. Owen paid for their dinner and left a nice tip. Scarlet then sidled up beside him as they headed for the street, which was bustling with Brooklyn hipsters.

"Let's get one more drink," Scarlet suggested, eager not to go home too soon. "Maybe at Ralph's?"

Owen nodded and turned the corner, heading for a bar in which they'd spent numerous wild nights. When they stepped through the doors, a familiar voice called Owen's name. It was Vincent, a film graduate from NYU. He hurried for them and wrapped an arm around Owen's shoulder.

"Dang, Owen! It's been a long time. Scarlet? Awesome to see the two of you."

Scarlet had always liked Vincent. In college, he'd made bizarre, science fiction short films that only a few people had liked. She hadn't seen him since he'd graduated, although she'd heard a rumor that he'd been making very cheap experimental music videos for music artists.

Owen and Scarlet ordered drinks, and Vincent beckoned for them to sit with him. Owen walked stiffly to the corner table, seemingly uninterested in him. Scarlet wondered why. *Was Owen just too successful in the film world to hang around with such "weird film experimentalists"?*

"Man, it's good to see you," Vincent repeated. "I just got back to New York after eight months abroad."

"Wow! What were you doing there?" Scarlet asked.

"I was working on a film," Vincent announced proudly. "Cinematography. It's just an indie thing. It won't have a wide release or whatever, but I should get to go to a few parties. There's been a bit of buzz around the screenwriter and the director as of late. Anyway, you know how these things go. The film won't be released for another two years or so."

"Right," Scarlet said. "I'm glad to hear it's going well!"

"Kind of a surprise, right? Nobody thought I would make anything useful," Vincent joked.

"I have to admit, that film you made about the life story of an ant was pretty experimental," Scarlet agreed.

"Ah, yes. The good old days." Vincent glanced up at Owen, who was quiet.

"Well, I dropped out of NYU," Scarlet announced, her voice heavy with irony.

"Oh, man. I hope you're okay?" Vincent asked.

"Sure. I'm fine. There's just a lot going on right now. We um. We got robbed."

Vincent's face lost its color. "That's insane, you guys. I keep hearing stories like that around the neighborhood. Are you okay? Did they take a lot of things?"

"It was quite a bit," Scarlet admitted. "But we weren't home when it happened, thank goodness. We're just reeling."

"I can't even imagine." Vincent again peered at Owen's face, hungry for him to say something. "I know things haven't been easy on you in general, Owen. It feels like the universe has it out for you."

*What did Vincent mean?* Scarlet glanced at Owen, whose cheek twitched.

"But I might have another project lined up for March," Vincent continued. "And they're looking for more help. People with film degrees and a bit of experience on set. The pay is pretty good, not great, but better than nothing. Should I pass your name along?"

Owen's eyes stirred with anger. Clearly, Vincent hadn't heard about Owen's incredible trajectory as a filmmaker.

"That's not necessary, Vincent," Owen said. "Thank you."

"It really isn't any trouble. You helped me out a time or two back in college. It's up to me to return the favor."

"Really. It's not necessary."

Owen was so humble. But Scarlet wanted Vincent to understand just how incredible her boyfriend was.

"Actually, Owen's being modest. He just got back today from a big film project in Los Angeles," Scarlet explained. "A forty-five-minute film with two or three mid-tier actors."

Owen didn't smile. Vincent's embarrassment was written across his face. He flashed Scarlet a strange look, then said, "Oh. Wow, man. I had no idea. Congratulations."

"Yep," Owen said, then drank from his beer.

"I mean, that's great. What lot were you filming on?"

"We were on location. In and around Joshua Tree," Owen explained.

"It's crazy hard to get a permit to film around Joshua Tree," Vincent said.

"Yeah. I have a great team. They helped with the logistics." Owen sounded bored, as though he'd explained this thousands of times.

Vincent's tone was strained. "You must be happy to have him back," he said to Scarlet.

"I do miss him a lot when he's gone," she said. "But I'm glad he gets to go after his dreams. It's rare that people are more art-driven than money-driven."

"You found yourself a good guy." Again, Vincent peered at Owen curiously. He then downed the rest of his drink and said he had to run. "But it was good to see you two."

After Vincent disappeared into the night, Scarlet leaned toward Owen and said, "That was weird."

Owen bristled. "I never really liked Vincent."

"But I'm glad he seems to be doing well," Scarlet said. "I mean, he's clearly clueless about how you're doing. But then again, he's been out of the country for a while. Maybe he's just out of touch."

"He always has been and always will be out of touch. Do you want another drink? I'm buying."

That night, Scarlet slipped beneath the sheets of the bed she'd shared with Owen for years. Owen had already slipped off to sleep, his eyes shifting gently beneath his eyelids. For a long time, Scarlet watched him sleep, overwhelmed with love for him.

But more than that, Scarlet had begun to burn with curiosity.

*Why had Vincent thought Owen wasn't at the top of his game?* Owen's career had been steadily climbing since his graduation from film school. His success was apparent. *Had someone told Vincent a different story? And if so, why had they lied about Owen's success?*

# Chapter Eight

Scarlet and her mother had begun to hate the chemo treatment center. The people who worked there had done very little to brighten the place up. It reeked of chemicals, its windows were lined with brown curtains, and its waiting area was decorated with posters that said, "Keep Your Chin Up" and "Hope Is The Greatest Cure Of All." Surprisingly, this was supposedly the very best chemo center in all of Manhattan. Scarlet didn't want to see the ones reserved for people with less money.

Then again, cancer didn't seem to care how much money you had. It took the rich, as well as the poor.

While Catherine received chemotherapy treatment, Scarlet stepped into the waiting area to grab a drink of water and text her siblings to make sure they were doing their homework. Ivy sent back an "eye roll" emoji, while James sent back a "thumbs up" emoji. A text then pinged in from Quentin, who said he was going to pick up Chinese that night for everyone. What was everyone's order?

Scarlet collapsed on a plastic chair and studied the

linoleum. Bored and frightened at once, she texted Owen to ask how his day was going. He sent back a photo of the omelet he'd cooked for himself, along with a "thumbs up" emoji. Scarlet smiled to herself, grateful he'd returned to the city.

It had been three nights since that mysterious interaction with Vincent. Since then, she and Owen had fallen into an easy rhythm, one of sleeping in too late, eating junk food, and laughing at YouTube videos. While Scarlet had checked in on her mother yesterday, Owen had met with another filmmaker to talk about future opportunities. Everything was headed in the right direction. Eventually, everything would be all right.

SCARLET: Omelet looks so YUMMY.

SCARLET: Did the insurance agent call you back?

As Scarlet waited for Owen's response, a middle-aged couple entered the waiting room. The man was timid, bald, and bleary-eyed from treatment. His wife wore a permanent frown. As they sat to wait to be called, they whispered intimately to one another. Scarlet heard one of them reference the "Hope Is The Greatest Cure Of All" poster, which made the other one laugh. It was clear that everyone hated the posters. They meant so little.

For the first time in a while, Scarlet went to Owen's Instagram. She hadn't been a big social media user as of late, as the feed normally showed her all the ways her life was falling apart. She wasn't in school. She wasn't at any cool parties. She wasn't super happy; she wasn't really fit.

Owen had posted three times in the past month. All three photos were taken in Los Angeles. In one, Owen had taken a selfie of just his eyes and the top of his head with the Santa Monica Pier behind him. In another, he stood to the left of a camera with his hands open— the typical director pose. The third photo was of a plate of seafood with the caption: "c'est la vie."

Scarlet breathed a sigh of relief. The photos upheld Owen's story. He'd clearly been in LA to work on a film.

Scarlet stood to check on her mother, who smiled a tired smile and said she was right as rain. "I just can't wait to get home and pile on the couch with you and Ivy."

Scarlet sat with Catherine a little while as her thoughts circled themselves. Was there something she was missing? As a journalist, Catherine had always said she needed to "trust her instincts." What were Scarlet's instincts? Could she trust them at all?

Feeling antsy, Scarlet headed to the bathroom, where she washed her face and hands. Afterward, she searched for the title of Owen's film online. Nothing came up. Then again, that didn't mean anything. As Vincent had said, films didn't come out for many years after they'd been made. Owen had just wrapped up filming. It would be months before he even teased the film.

Again, Scarlet found herself planted on the partial selfie of Owen's face. It had been posted about three weeks ago, and Scarlet had "liked" it at the time, along with seventy-eight other people. Owen was well-liked; his social media reflected that.

Under the photograph, three people had commented. A guy Scarlet had met in Owen's film school had put a "sunshine" emoji. Another had written, "Looking good, man." And a third had written, "You're so lucky to feel that sun on your face."

*Huh.* There was something odd about that comment. *Wasn't there?* It sounded almost sarcastic. Scarlet leaned against the bathroom wall and clicked on the profile of the commenter, who was a woman named @tiffbunny. *Tiff Bunny? Tiffany Bunny?* Scarlet's heart began to pound.

Tiffany was a bombshell blond with very long, sculpted legs and a propensity for posting selfies with duckfaces. In several, she had a sucker in her mouth. She wore beautiful and thick winter scarves and had a well-lit apartment in Queens that was decorated with Scandinavian minimalism. She was everything Scarlet hated about Instagram, as she reminded Scarlet of just how much she lacked.

*But how did Tiffany know Owen?* Scarlet headed back through Tiffany's timeline to hunt for clues. More than a year passed before she got her answer. Owen had directed a music video for Tiffany's solo music, one that featured Tiffany with a guitar all over Brooklyn, Manhattan, and Queens. Scarlet had seen some of the video footage at the time and had been very proud of Owen's advancements. Tiffany's beauty had initially troubled Scarlet, but she'd soon shoved those thoughts away. *What was any relationship without trust?*

If there was anything her parents had taught her, it was that love was built on trust. Quentin Copperfield was a lot of things — selfish, arrogant, and career-driven, to name a few, but he was also overwhelmingly in love with his wife. Scarlet had always wanted a love like that.

Scarlet returned to the top of Tiffany's feed, nearly ready to shove her phone in her pocket and dismiss her "instincts." But just before she closed Tiffany's feed, something caught her eye. In the corner of the third photo on Tiffany's timeline— hardly visible, really, if you weren't looking hard enough— was a pair of boots.

Scarlet clicked through the photo and studied the boots. For many moments, she forgot to breathe.

The boots were Owen's. She would have recognized them anywhere. They'd picked them out together at a second-hand place in Brooklyn on a rainy day in late October when Owen had joked that he wanted to go more "lumberjack" with his style. The boots had been made in Norway and cost seventy-seven dollars. When he'd packed them to go to Los Angeles,

Scarlet had teased him. "I can't go anywhere without my boots," he'd said.

But in this photo, Owen's boots weren't in Los Angeles. They were in Queens.

Scarlet scrambled for answers. The photo was uploaded on a day he was supposedly filming in California. It was possible Tiffany had uploaded the photo later than it had been taken. *But if that was true, why hadn't Owen mentioned his friendship with Tiffany?* Scarlet always told him where she was and who she'd seen— not because he expected her to, but because she had nothing to hide. *Did he do the same?*

Scarlet's vision was blurry. She clicked out of Instagram, put her phone away, and tumbled into the waiting room. Should she call Owen? Something told her not to. Something told her to take the photo of the boots seriously. Something told her it was very wrong.

To Scarlet's surprise, there was a familiar figure in the waiting area. Quentin hovered in the center of the room, switching his weight from foot to foot. He looked strange and out of sorts, as though his eyes couldn't make sense of anything they saw. His hair was greasy, and his clothes looked like they didn't fit him properly.

"Dad?" Scarlet had never seen Quentin look so disheveled and out of sorts.

Suddenly, Quentin turned to look at her. His eyes looked lost. He staggered toward her, but soon collapsed on a plastic chair. Tears welled in his eyes. *Was he drunk?*

"Dad, what the heck is wrong with you?" Scarlet was surprised at how angry she sounded. In truth, she was scared.

Quentin's face twisted into a red and blotchy mess.

Scarlet hurried to the chair beside him. Embarrassed, she hissed, "Dad, if you can't keep it together, you have to wait outside."

But Quentin was long gone. His sobs echoed through the

waiting room. One teenage girl in the corner peered at them curiously, too sick to care that staring was rude. Quentin dropped his head on Scarlet's shoulder and shook with sorrow.

What on earth could Scarlet do but hold onto him for dear life and whisper, "It's going to be all right, Dad." What on earth could she do but lie?

# Chapter Nine

It took every bit of strength Scarlet had to get both of her parents out of the chemo clinic and into the waiting car. Catherine was very tired, so much so that Scarlet requested a wheelchair to wheel her outside. As they went, Quentin continued to blubber, frequently pausing to lean against the wall and weep into his hand. Scarlet hadn't gotten any information out of him. The soft smell of alcohol on his breath told her everything she needed to know. Like so many people in America, he'd lost track of his life— and he'd turned to the bar for comfort. Great. Like Scarlet didn't have enough problems. She was just grateful Catherine seemed too tired to notice.

In the car, Scarlet made heavy eye contact with the driver, who nodded in understanding. He saw what state Quentin was in, and he was just as worried as she was. When they reached the apartment building, Scarlet watched as Quentin stepped from the car and then turned to help Catherine onto the sidewalk.

"What happened to him?" Scarlet hissed.

"I'm not sure. He didn't need me all day, and then suddenly, I got a call." The driver spoke very delicately, frightened his boss would overhear. "The leave of absence has really taken a toll on his already fragile state. Do you have someone you can call? Someone to help?"

Scarlet closed her eyes. Who could she possibly reach out to? Catherine's sister had left New York City several years ago to follow her new husband to Dubai. All of Quentin's family lived on the island of Nantucket, and Scarlet had never met them before. Besides, Quentin's relationship with them was tenuous, at best. He would never forgive her for reaching out.

*Who else? Anyone in Manhattan?* Quentin and Catherine's friends were all in the "scene" of the Upper West Side and would view Scarlet's request for help as ultimate gossip. This could destroy Quentin's reputation even more. Scarlet didn't want to take the fall for that.

"I can handle it," Scarlet told the driver with a firm nod. "Thank you for your help today."

The doorman greeted them. "Good evening, Copperfield family." He even pressed the button on the elevator for them, sensing things were a bit off. Once they got in the elevator, Catherine placed her head tenderly on Quentin's arm, and tears raced down Quentin's cheek. All Scarlet wanted in the world was to call Owen to ask him to come to help her. But with the sudden onslaught of potential information, she was stunted. *Maybe Owen was a stranger.*

The living room was chaos. Ivy and James had had friends over from apartments on lower floors, and pizza boxes were strewn across the coffee tables and couch cushions. Scarlet was pretty sure she saw Ivy hide a bottle of vodka behind a plant but felt too tired to care.

"Guys? I need everyone whose last name isn't Copperfield to clear out." Scarlet pointed at the elevator.

One after another, the teenagers who didn't belong to them

shoved on their shoes, grabbed the last slices of pizza, and raced for the elevator. Meanwhile, Ivy busied herself with pouting about "never seeing her friends" as James realized something was very wrong with their parents.

"Ivy?" James muttered.

"What?" Ivy turned toward him, enraged.

"Ivy, I think we should go to our rooms." James nodded toward Quentin, who stumbled down the hallway.

All the color drained from Ivy's cheeks. She locked eyes with Scarlet. "Scar? What is wrong with Dad?"

"Everyone's just exhausted," Scarlet explained as she guided their mother to the bedroom. "I think it'll be an early night for all of us. Do you mind cleaning up the pizza boxes before you go?"

It was bizarre to make sure her parents were put to bed, as though they'd very quickly switched places. Both Quentin and Catherine fell asleep very quickly and left Scarlet in the soft haze of their gray-lit bedroom. Scarlet tip-toed back to the living room to find it empty, with only a few crumbs scattered across the coffee table. For the first time in a half hour, she recognized the state of her own anxiety. It was through the roof.

In the refrigerator, Scarlet found an old bottle of unopened white wine. It had probably been there since before Catherine's diagnosis. After she poured herself a glass, she grabbed her phone and sent a text off to Owen, deciding to face the monster upfront.

SCARLET: Hey! Do you know someone named Tiffany?

Almost immediately, she dropped the phone on the counter, terrified of what she'd done. She took a long drink from her wine and watched the text message, waiting for Owen to read it. But a minute passed, then another. The text message was not only not read; it seemed like it hadn't even been sent.

"What the heck?" Scarlet muttered, confused. Normally, she had great service in the apartment. *Was there an outage?*

To test her service, she texted Alyssa, who was on Martha's Vineyard.

SCARLET: Hey, girl! How are you doing?

ALYSSA: Omg! Hi! It's so good to hear from you. I'm doing well, although it's so cold here. Like, single digits. Grandma Nancy and I spent the evening drinking hot toddies to beat the cold.

ALYSSA: How are you? Have you and Owen figured out the insurance situation yet? Sounds like such a nightmare.

Scarlet's heart thumped. Clearly, her phone service wasn't the problem. It had something to do with Owen's phone. Perhaps he'd let the battery die out. Perhaps he'd turned it off to focus on work. Or perhaps... No. She didn't want to consider any other options.

But Alyssa's question had triggered a memory. Back when Scarlet and Owen had first gotten the apartment, Scarlet had really wanted to get out from under her father's thumb, so much so that she hadn't wanted to put her last name on any documents. As she'd spent her entire life as Quentin Copperfield's daughter, she was worried the mere mention of "Copperfield" would change things for landlords or insurance providers. "If people know you come from money, they take advantage of you," she'd told Owen. "And I just want to be me. I want to be Scarlet from Brooklyn."

Because of this, Scarlet had asked Owen to put everything

in his name. The apartment. The insurance. Everything. She hadn't even considered he would take advantage of her. They were in love.

Scarlet started to panic. She paced the living room, remembering the night she'd discovered they'd been robbed. The first thing she'd done was call Owen. He'd been so kind, so understanding. He'd asked her to knock on the neighbor's door for protection. He'd thought of her well-being above all else.

*But was it an act? Had Owen actually been in Los Angeles at all?* Vincent certainly hadn't thought Owen was working on anything film related. Scarlet needed to find another source.

Over the years, Scarlet had met many of Owen's friends. One of them, another filmmaker named Chelsea, had always been kind to Scarlet, asking her questions about her schooling and telling her not to take anything too seriously yet. She was too young.

Scarlet called Chelsea's cell. Chelsea's raspy New Jersey accent answered with a mix of surprise and happiness. "Scarlet Copperfield! To what do I owe the honor of your call?"

"Chelsea, I'm so glad you answered." Scarlet sounded a lot more frantic than she wanted to.

"Is there something wrong?"

"Um. I was curious. When was the last time you saw Owen?"

"Oh, God. Is he okay? Is he missing?"

"No. Nothing like that." *Or was he? Had he gone missing?* "I just can't get a hold of him right now, and I'm worried. We were robbed a couple of weeks ago, and I'm thinking we've been, like, targeted or something."

"Jeez. Robbed? I'm so sorry, Scarlet. I keep hearing stories like that around the city. It's terrifying."

"It really is," Scarlet said.

"Well, the last I heard, Owen was out in LA," Chelsea said.

"Yes! LA. He told you about that?" Scarlet was suddenly overjoyed. She was worried about nothing.

"He mentioned it, yeah. Some film project."

"He didn't tell you anything else?" Scarlet's joy waned.

"Erm. No." Chelsea fumbled over her words. "I mean, no specifics."

Scarlet's ears were ringing.

"But I was happy for him, even if it was just a weekend gig," Chelsea explained.

*A weekend gig.* Scarlet's eyes closed at the finality of the statement. In the version Owen had given her, his film project had taken weeks. It had filmed in Joshua Tree. It had caused a monumental shift in his film career.

"Chelsea? You don't have to answer this. But do you know if Owen is cheating on me?" Scarlet could barely hear herself speak.

Chelsea was quiet for a moment. Scarlet was embarrassed, yet she felt she had no other choice.

"I don't know if Owen is cheating on you," Chelsea said finally. "I just know it wouldn't be the first time Owen has cheated. He has a history."

Scarlet was stunned into silence. A thousand memories filled her brain— morning kisses, whispered words, long walks through the city, shared pieces of toast. The tiny moments had meant so much to her. *Had they meant anything to him?*

"Thank you for telling me the truth, Chelsea," Scarlet whispered.

"Of course. It's girl code, isn't it?" Chelsea sighed. "Listen, you're still young. If you have a hunch that Owen is being unfaithful, then there's no reason you should stay with him. Take some time for yourself. Consider what you want out of life."

Scarlet couldn't bear to listen to another piece of advice. Midway through Chelsea's monologue, Scarlet hung up the phone. Again, she stared at the message she'd sent Owen, which still hadn't gone through. Had he blocked her? *Was that even possible?*

Suddenly, Scarlet heard her mother's voice calling her name. Scarlet bolted to the bedroom to help her mother from bed. Slowly but urgently, she guided her mother to the bathroom, where she vomited. Scarlet's eyes were heavy with tears. On the other side of the bed, Quentin continued to sleep off the alcohol, safe from the world for a little while.

Scarlet needed help. She needed help desperately.

When she finally got her mother back to bed, Scarlet poured herself another glass of wine and stared obsessively at Tiffany's Instagram for a full ten minutes. She wanted the never-ending stream of photos to show her something concrete about Owen's cheating. It was like looking for landmines. But, if Tiffany really was Owen's other girlfriend, she'd been very careful to conceal him.

This led Scarlet to another fear. What if Scarlet was the "other" girlfriend, and Tiffany was the real one? For years, Owen had called Scarlet "bunny" as a nickname. Tiffany's Instagram name was @tiffbunny. *What were the odds?*

Suddenly, the doorbell intercom buzzed. Scarlet leaped to her feet and answered the call.

"Hello? Copperfield residence?"

"Hi, Scarlet. I hope you got your parents to bed all right."

"I did, thank you." The doormen saw and knew everything about the people in their buildings. It was a fact of the city.

"I have two people down here who say they know your father," the doorman continued. "Their names are Bernard and Greta Copperfield. Should I let them come up?"

Scarlet's jaw dropped. Bernard and Greta Copperfield were her grandparents— she knew that much. Beyond that, she'd been able to follow the drama surrounding Bernard's release from prison and his subsequent "innocence" in public opinion. Despite his rugged and aging face, Quentin looked so much like his father.

If she saw them up close, she would know it was them. But after the robbery, she wasn't willing to bring anyone up the elevator. It wasn't safe.

"I'll be right down," Scarlet told the doorman. "Thank you."

# Chapter Ten

Scarlet held her breath all the way to the bottom floor. When the elevator doors parted, she stepped into the warm glow of the lobby, where the doorman stood at the front desk and conversed with two people in their late sixties or early seventies. The couple wore beautiful wool coats and warm hats, and their skin was soft and pink from the chill of the February air. As they spoke with the doorman, their eyes were open and eager, as though they hung from his every word. As Scarlet approached, she learned the doorman spoke only about his daughter and her newfound quest to be an Olympic gymnast.

"You can't let her give up on her dreams," the older woman said sternly, as though they spoke about something way more important than childhood gymnastics. "The way your children think about their dreams now sets the stage for the rest of their lives."

"I feel the same way," the doorman said. "I think it's the greatest privilege in the world to guide our young people through their childhood."

"It's a privilege, yes," the older woman said.

"When they hit their teenage years, it's a whole other mountain to climb. But Greta and I never regretted a thing," the older man explained as he took his wife's hand.

"How many children did you raise?" the doorman asked.

"Four. Three daughters and one son," Greta explained. "Like we said, our eldest lives here."

"Quentin Copperfield," Bernard finished.

"Hello?" Scarlet's timid voice barely crossed the lobby. She clasped her hands together nervously as Bernard and Greta Copperfield turned toward her. Together, they were an immaculate couple— a handsome and sturdy man with grizzled hair and a big collection of sweaters and books, alongside a pristine and beautiful woman whose skin glowed peaches and cream even into her seventieth year. Scarlet, who'd never known a single grandparent, could hardly believe her eyes. Would they recognize her as one of their own? Would they accept her as a grandchild?

"Oh. Goodness. You must be Scarlet." Greta's voice was filled with love. She took several steps forward but paused in the middle of the lobby, as though she didn't want to frighten Scarlet away.

"How could you tell?" Scarlet asked.

Bernard stepped forward to join Greta. "You've got that Copperfield look to you. What did Quentin say you are, now? Twenty-two?"

"That's right," Scarlet whispered. She eyed the doorman, who listened intently as she met her family for the first time. It was an intimate moment. "My siblings are eighteen and sixteen. Ivy and James."

Greta's eyes pooled with tears, but she seemed adamant not to let them fall.

"I'm sorry I didn't let you come upstairs at first," Scarlet began. "I'm in charge of the house right now, and I didn't want to let just anyone up."

"We could have been just anyone," Bernard agreed. "It was good of you to come downstairs first."

Greta took another tentative step forward, fishing through her purse for her wallet. Finally, she snapped it open to leaf out a very old photograph, which she passed to Scarlet. In it, a young woman who could only have been Greta sat on a sofa next to a man who could only have been Bernard. In Greta's arms was a baby with jet-black hair.

Scarlet was shocked to the core. "Is this my dad?"

Greta nodded. "It doesn't prove anything, of course. But I thought maybe you'd never seen your father as a baby before."

"I never had," Scarlet affirmed. "He was really cute."

"He was. But don't tell him that," Bernard teased. "I used to be able to carry him with one hand."

Scarlet sniffed and smiled. Up close, her grandparents' wrinkles were deeper, and the gray of their hair was starker. She loved their imperfections all the more. *Was this what it was like to get old with someone? To love them for what society called their "flaws"?* She could have grown to love Owen's flaws. She'd already fallen for his snoring and how he couldn't pronounce any Spanish words correctly. She'd wanted to find out what flaws awaited them in the future.

"Let's go upstairs," Scarlet said, waving at the doorman to show everything was okay. "I can make some tea."

"Tea sounds incredible," Greta agreed.

In the elevator, Scarlet stood behind Greta and Bernard.

"What a lovely apartment building," Greta said. "Bernard, you didn't tell me how nice it was."

"You've been here before?" Scarlet asked.

"Just a couple of times," Bernard explained. "I was on my book tour and stopped by to see your father."

Scarlet's grandfather had been to her family's apartment yet hadn't been introduced to her. This filled her heart with a strange longing for a time she would never get back. Perhaps, like Alyssa, she should have spent time on the New England island with her grandparents. Perhaps she should have learned how to sail, spent hours building sandcastles, and had an island romance.

The elevator doors opened onto their apartment. Scarlet watched Greta's expression as they stepped into the immaculate space, with its floor-to-ceiling windows that reflected back a gorgeous view of Manhattan. Pizza crumbs from Ivy and James's little party still lined the coffee table, but Greta didn't mention them. Instead, she said, "Wow. What a place to grow up. It must have felt like a dream."

"In some ways, it was," Scarlet explained. "But I'm sure growing up on Nantucket was a different kind of dream."

Greta and Bernard exchanged painful expressions.

"I'm sure your father never really talks about it," Bernard said.

"And there's no blaming Quentin for that," Greta continued. "Our family had a very difficult twenty-five years. We're only now picking up the pieces."

Scarlet stepped around the island and began to prepare tea for the three of them. As she worked, Greta and Bernard sat on the stools surrounding the island and spoke quietly about their trip from Nantucket. Apparently, they'd left in the early afternoon and alternated driving, which had reminded them of long-ago drives they'd taken as newlyweds.

"It's funny. I'm seventy now, but my life has felt like a blink in time. Maybe you know this, and maybe you don't. But I met your grandfather in Paris when the two of us were twenty-something and very susceptible to falling in love," Greta said.

Scarlet placed steaming mugs of green tea in front of both of them and tried, yet failed, to imagine the two of them in their twenties. That was one of the worst problems with human imagination, she thought. It was almost impossible to see how anyone or anything looked outside of a given time.

"Paris sounds like a dream," Scarlet said.

"Have you been?" Bernard asked.

"My mother took Ivy and I when I was eighteen and Ivy was fourteen. Ivy and I both loved shopping for clothes, but our mother made us do tons of cultural things while we were there. Looking back, I'm grateful she did that. I would never have forced myself into the Louvre, but I'm grateful we went. You know?"

Greta and Bernard nodded.

"Your mother sounds like a remarkable woman," Greta said softly. "I can't believe I've never met her. I did, of course, google her. Some of the articles she wrote popped up. She is really an incredible writer. No— it's more than that. She's an exceptional storyteller. She knows exactly what questions to ask to draw the story out of whoever she interviews. It's a rare thing for a journalist."

"And one your father doesn't always master," Bernard said mischievously.

Greta smacked Bernard on the wrist.

"No. It's okay," Scarlet said quickly. "My dad is always quick to point out that Mom is the better journalist. She just never wanted the limelight the way he did." Scarlet paused for a moment, searching her memories. "The weird thing is, I don't think Dad is jealous about that. He genuinely loves her work. And he hates that his star power has changed the way my mother can engage with her work."

"Oh, dear." Greta furrowed her brows, then glanced at Bernard.

"Your grandmother is looking at me like that because we had a similar dynamic," Bernard explained. "She was always the more brilliant one. And I was always eager for more star power."

Scarlet was surprised at how easy it was to speak with her grandparents. She indulged in the warmth of her tea, and the tension in her shoulders loosened. For the first time that day, other adults were in the room, prepared to take control. For the first time, Owen's cheating wasn't at the forefront of her mind.

"Scarlet. Do you mind if we ask you about your father?" Bernard spoke timidly.

What answers could Scarlet give them? She didn't understand her father at all.

"When I saw him in December, he was quite upset. He told me about your mother, which is just terrible. I can't tell you how sorry we are," Bernard continued. "But since then, he's hardly communicated with us. Our eldest daughter, Alana, sometimes gets through to him, but their conversations are brief and don't give us any insight into how he is."

"We were happy to see him on the news the past month or so since it confirmed he was at least well enough to read the news. But when Jackson Crawford took over his nightly news slot, we got worried," Greta said.

"Jackson Crawford is your ex-uncle," Bernard said. "Your Aunt Julia's ex-husband, that is."

"And a monster." Greta's eyes flashed.

"She doesn't use that word lightly," Bernard explained.

Scarlet was overwhelmed. This was a lot of information at once. She'd heard the name "Jackson Crawford" across the city since he'd overtaken her father's news slot. But never in her wildest dreams could she have imagined he was her ex-uncle. *How small was the world, anyway?*

"So. We're here." Bernard paused. "Where is your father, anyway?"

Suddenly, the hallway floorboard creaked. Scarlet raised her head to watch her father slump through the shadows. He seemed to have more control over his body than he had hours before, and his eyes were more-or-less clear. Scarlet was glad to see he'd put on a pair of sweatpants and a t-shirt. She wasn't sure how she could explain that he'd taken to sleeping in his clothes.

"Oh. Quentin." Greta stood from the stool and rushed for her son. In a moment, her arms were around him, and Quentin's were around her. Quentin's eyes closed as he held onto his much smaller mother for dear life. Meanwhile, Bernard stepped up beside him and placed his hand on Quentin's shoulder. Step-by-step, they guided him to the couch, where they sat on either side of him.

"What are you doing here?" Quentin finally asked.

Greta wrapped a strand of his dark hair around his ear. "We wanted to come and check on you, honey."

"You shouldn't be here." Quentin didn't sound angry. His words were matter-of-fact.

"Darling, we had to find out if you were all right," Greta returned with the same amount of stubbornness.

Quentin let out a single sob. Greta rubbed his upper back.

"You shouldn't have come. I never came to check on you," Quentin mumbled. His shame seemed to echo through the living room. Scarlet understood that whatever drama existed between her and her father was nothing compared to the mountain of drama between Quentin and his parents.

"Shh. That's in the past now. We're moving forward. As a family," Greta whispered. "But you have to let us help you."

Quentin dropped his head onto Greta's shoulder. Scarlet had never seen him so defeated. As Greta pressed her hand over Quentin's forehead, Bernard turned and beckoned for Scarlet to come join them. But Scarlet wasn't sure she could. This wasn't the father she knew.

"Why don't you run to bed?" Greta urged. "You've been holding down the fort for too long, my dear. Let us take over for a little while."

"Do you still have a room here? Somewhere you can

sleep?" Bernard asked. He seemed to know she no longer lived at home. Had Quentin told him how much he hated Scarlet's boyfriend?

At this, Quentin interjected. "She still has a room here. She will always have a room here." But he still didn't have the strength to turn around and face her. Scarlet froze at his words. They were immediate and heavy with regret and love. Urged by her grandmother, Scarlet finally took the route back to her bedroom. There, she collapsed at the edge of the bed and sat in the dark for a full five minutes, thinking of the harshness of the world. It never seemed to get any easier.

# Chapter Eleven

It was surreal to have Greta and Bernard Copperfield in his living room. Quentin felt as though he'd emerged from a stupor to discover them, and now, as his consciousness returned, he found himself gaining strength. Even his voice sounded like his own, surer of itself. There was a strength in his first nuclear family, one Quentin had refused to acknowledge until now. He was glad they'd come.

The clock on the wall read twelve-thirty. Still, his seventy-something parents were wide-eyed and eager to sit with him to hear how he was doing. As a parent, Quentin could understand this. If Scarlet was going through something traumatic, he would find the strength to sit with her all night long to get to the bottom of the issue. He would do anything to help her.

Quentin was not proud of how the day had gone. That morning, the doctor had called Catherine and Quentin into his office to discuss the chemo treatment and his belief that a double mastectomy was best. Catherine's fear and sorrow had doubled; her grip around Quentin's hand had intensified so much that Quentin was reminded of all three times she'd given birth. After the meeting with the doctor, Catherine had assured Quentin they should keep up the day's schedule; that Scarlet should bring her to chemotherapy, like always. *"I need my daughter with me today. We can deal with the surgery topic later."*

How had Quentin ended up at the bar in Midtown? How many gin and tonics had he drunk? He'd found himself washed up, career-less, his wife exhausted from chemotherapy and on the verge of a dramatic surgery, and his daughter hating him. Quentin Copperfield had once been a great man, but he no longer recognized himself. How could he go on?

"Why did you come today?" Quentin asked, rubbing his temples.

Greta and Bernard exchanged glances.

"We've been worried about you for almost two months now," Greta breathed. "Well, that's not true. If I'm honest, I've worried about you since the day you were born. You're a parent, though. You understand how that goes."

Quentin nodded. Worry was one thing in this world he understood.

"The doctor said Catherine needs a double mastectomy," Quentin muttered.

"Goodness," Greta said.

Bernard rubbed his back. "You just learned this today?"

"Yes. We haven't told the kids yet. Every day, this disease and its treatment seems to get worse. I don't know how much I can handle." He paused, then added, "And I'm not even the sick one."

"You're doing your best to carry it on your own," Greta assured him.

"Scarlet's been such a huge help," Quentin added. "She hates my guts, but she's been there for her mother. Catherine says it's only a phase. That she'll find a way to like me again. But I don't know. This has been a pretty long phase."

"Scarlet is here, isn't she?" Bernard reminded him. "She's asleep in that room down the hall. If she really hated you, she wouldn't be here."

"You're a Copperfield. You should know better than most that families don't get along all the time." Greta's voice was very soft and tentative.

Quentin bowed his head, suddenly overwhelmed with the idea that Scarlet would soon come back to him. He couldn't push her. He had to wait.

"About this surgery," Bernard said. "Why don't you let me make a few phone calls? Greta and I had a dear friend at the Sorbonne who went on to be one of the most celebrated surgeons in all of Manhattan."

"Oh, yes. Mark was about as smart as they come. He was the only scientist we let into the fold, you know. He always asked me what good all my reading and writing would do for the world. I suppose he was right about that," Greta said.

Quentin bristled. "Is this another of your friends who abandoned you after the trial?"

Bernard's face grew shadowed. Immediately, Quentin regretted what he'd said.

"I'm sorry," Quentin muttered. "Gosh, I'm sorry."

"No. It's a valid question," Bernard said. "I haven't been so keen to call any of the friends who were quick to drop me in the nineties. But I assure you, Mark wasn't one of them. We'd already lost track of each other by then due to his incredibly busy schedule here in Manhattan."

"I see," Quentin said, although he wasn't sure he believed his father. He was surprised at how angry he was at anyone who'd wronged him.

"Let me make a few phone calls tomorrow morning," Bernard urged. "I promise you that Mark is the best in the business. I would trust him with the life of anyone I hold dear. I don't know Catherine, nor anyone in your family. It's one of my greatest sorrows." Bernard paused and gazed intently at the window, where late-night Manhattan lights glittered. "But I hope to know all of them soon."

Quentin felt the question coming like a storm.

"How long will you be off the air?" Bernard asked.

Quentin shrugged. "I assume you saw Jackson Crawford in my chair."

"Terrible. Just terrible," Greta grunted. "I thank the stars above that Julia isn't married to that man anymore."

"They've told me he's just a temporary fill-in," Quentin continued. "But if he does well, I don't see why he wouldn't take over my chair. This is how I got the desk seventeen years ago. I worked extremely hard and proved myself when others couldn't handle the position."

"That desk is yours," Greta reminded him. "The entire country looks to Quentin Copperfield for the nightly news. Jackson Crawford just doesn't have what you have."

Quentin wanted to remind his mother that she was biased. She was his mother, after all.

"But why don't you come to Nantucket for a while?" Bernard said, just as Quentin had known he would. "Take a break from this scenery."

"Dad..." Quentin warned. "Our lives are here. That brilliant surgeon of yours is here. I can't just uproot my family and take off for some seaside paradise."

"And why not?" Bernard demanded. "Just as you say, it is paradise. In the olden days, doctors sent their patients to the seaside for the clean air. Why not bring Catherine?"

"You don't have to decide right away," Greta chimed in. "But The Copperfield House has enough space for you and your entire family. Alana, Julia, Ella, and I would love to help your wife as she heals. And Nantucket High School is a remarkable place. One of the top journalists in the United States graduated from there, you know."

Quentin rolled his eyes, even as a smile played across his lips.

"Just come for a few months and see how you like it," Bernard pressed him. "Your family needs extra support right now. And that eldest daughter of yours looks too exhausted to carry the weight of this for a moment more."

Slowly, Quentin felt himself nod in agreement. His parents were right; he couldn't live as he always had any longer. The rules of the universe had changed, and he needed to adapt.

"I'll call the girls in the morning," Greta said. "They'll prepare your rooms."

And just like that, the decision was final. The next generation of Copperfields was heading to Nantucket.

# Chapter Twelve

For the first time in years, Scarlet woke up at her parents' apartment. As she lay in the gray shadows, a February rain pattered against the windowpane, and the smell of eggs and pancakes came under the crack in the doorway. It was seven-thirty, fifteen minutes before Ivy and James needed to head to high school. *Had someone cooked them breakfast?*

Scarlet rubbed her eyes and walked slowly toward the kitchen. There, a bright-eyed Greta Copperfield flipped over-easy eggs onto two plates and shimmied sausages and pancakes onto a larger serving plate. Both Ivy and James were dressed and seated at the island, beaming at their grandmother, who they'd probably never seen before. Bernard placed orange juices in front of them and explained, "Nobody in the world makes a better breakfast than Greta Copperfield. It looks simple— but I promise you, she adds just a touch of something magical that makes the food stick to your bones that much longer."

"I can't believe you're here," Ivy interjected. "Did my dad call you?"

Greta and Bernard exchanged glances. "He did, actually," Greta lied. "We made it clear to him we wanted to help your family out as much as we could."

"Good," James snorted. "We clearly needed help!"

"Did you guys sleep at all?" Scarlet asked, surprising everyone with her presence.

Ivy jumped. "Scar! You never sleep over." She looked pleased.

"It got late," Scarlet tried to explain.

"It's good you slept here," Greta assured her, reaching into the fridge to grab a couple more eggs. "I can't imagine what it's like to travel back to Brooklyn every night. It must feel so lonely."

"She lives with her boyfriend," Ivy bragged. "He's a filmmaker."

"Isn't that something," Bernard said. "The Copperfields are always drawn to people in the arts."

Scarlet's eyes watered. She did not want to think about Owen, not even for a moment.

"Grab a seat, honey," Greta said. "Do you have any classes today at NYU?"

Scarlet blushed and perched on a stool next to her sister. After a very dramatic pause, she surprised herself with the truth. "I dropped out this semester, actually."

Ivy's jaw dropped.

"What?" James leaned over his plate of eggs to gape at her.

But behind the counter, Greta and Bernard hardly paused in their breakfast preparations.

"It's a very difficult time," Greta said breezily. "I can't imagine it's easy to think clearly. You all have so much on your plates."

"Yeah. I was wasting everyone's time," Scarlet explained.

"The semester had only just begun, and already, my professors were frustrated. Besides, I'm a senior, and I still don't know what I'm majoring in. I have no direction!"

Bernard stood with his own plate of eggs and circled his fork through the air thoughtfully. "I think being directionless at twenty-two is a gift, Scarlet."

Greta nodded. "Every single possibility is still open for you! You can be whatever you want to be. You can study languages or write poetry or move to Sardinia to raise cattle or—"

Scarlet laughed, surprised at how simple this all was to her grandparents. "I don't know about that last one. But maybe you're right."

"We've lived long enough to have made every single mistake," Greta explained.

"Just don't tell my father yet," Scarlet said under her breath. "He's angry enough with me as it is." She flashed dark glances to both of her siblings, who nodded in agreement.

"I won't be the one to tell him," Ivy joked. "I don't have a death wish."

A few minutes later, Scarlet, Greta, and Bernard got the two high school students out the door. Afterward, Scarlet urged Greta to serve herself some breakfast and take a breather so that Scarlet could get started on the dishes. Bernard scrubbed the countertops and spoke about the joys of Nantucket in the springtime, which was really just around the corner.

"It'll be my first transition from winter to spring since I got out of prison," he explained. "This year, I'm trying not to take anything for granted. I will stop and gaze at every sunset. I will observe every new bud on a tree."

"It sounds like a magical place," Scarlet said.

"Oh, it is." Greta smiled and tapped a napkin over her lips.

That morning, something incredible happened. It was as though, after so many months of aimlessness, sorrow, and fear, the Copperfields learned to strengthen themselves for the next phase of their lives together.

Quentin and Catherine woke up not long after the teenagers left for school. Catherine was tired and hollow, but her smile warmed up the room. "Thank you for getting my kids out the door," she said as she wrapped herself in a blanket on the couch. Scarlet wrapped up beside her, grateful to have her close, as Quentin, Greta, and Bernard sat around the living room with cups of coffee.

"Thank you for sticking around last night," Quentin said tenderly to Scarlet.

Scarlet nodded. She didn't want to tell him the truth— that she wasn't sure she had anywhere to go. She'd texted Owen ten more times and called him twice. It was clear there was something very wrong, something she didn't fully want to acknowledge yet.

Over the next few minutes, Catherine and Quentin explained the next phase of Catherine's treatment. The words "double mastectomy" terrified Scarlet, even as Catherine tried to assure her that it was definitely the right move.

"And your grandfather knows the best surgeon for the job here in Manhattan," Quentin continued.

Scarlet blinked up at Bernard. For months in the media, she'd read about this "intellectual giant, Bernard Copperfield." Now, she saw him only as her cozy and friendly grandfather.

"I'm going to be okay," Catherine whispered, taking Scarlet's hand. "I'm going to keep fighting this, just like always."

"And the surgery will be a big help," Quentin added. "I just got off the phone with the surgeon. He can fit your mother in next week."

Scarlet's breath came in starts and stops. Still, she had to believe these people. They were all she had left.

"After that, we're going to spend some time on Nantucket," Quentin explained. "I think it'll be good for all of us to take time to heal. Of course, you're twenty-two and have a million responsibilities here in the city, along with a boyfriend and an apartment of your own. But I hope you'll find time to come out to see us on the island."

Scarlet's throat was tight with sorrow. Now was probably the time to tell him about Owen, about the robbery, and about dropping out of NYU. But how could she disappoint him so much all at once?

"I'd love to visit," Scarlet said instead. "It sounds like the perfect retreat."

* * *

That afternoon, as Greta and Bernard took a much-needed nap and Quentin and Catherine retreated to their bedroom, Scarlet headed into the shattering cold to investigate her Brooklyn apartment and the last dregs of her relationship. It thrilled her to think of storming in to scream at Owen, to ask why he respected her so little, and to demand he give her the money from the insurance. The love from her family had given her strength.

But as she neared the apartment, Scarlet got more and more nervous. What did she actually know about this guy? Yes, she'd lived with him for a couple years. Yes, she'd loved him. But now that he'd expunged her from his life weeks after the robbery, he seemed calculating and manipulative. *What was he capable of? Was he violent, too?* She couldn't rule it out.

Alyssa was back that afternoon from Martha's Vineyard and agreed to meet Scarlet outside the apartment building. When Scarlet explained the gist of what she'd learned and what she suspected, Alyssa's face grew stony with rage. She'd been through her own troubles with men over the years, and she had no patience for it.

"Listen to me. You do not deserve this," Alyssa blared,

squeezing Scarlet's arms a little too hard. "You gave him your time, your love, and your commitment."

"Yeah. I'm a great judge of character, aren't I?"

"Don't be hard on yourself," Alyssa urged. "You did the best you could with the information you had. But times have changed. Let's go up there and tell that idiot what's what."

At the door, Scarlet's hand shook as she tried to put the key into the lock. Alyssa ultimately took over, shoving it in violently. When she tried to turn it, however, it didn't work.

"Are you sure it's the right key?" Alyssa asked.

Scarlet double-checked. "That's the key, all right."

Alyssa's cheeks were red with anger. "He must have changed the lock."

"How could he do that?" Scarlet felt dizzy with fear. She hurried down the staircase and grabbed her phone, searching for answers. Alyssa raced after her, muttering to herself.

A minute later, her landlord answered her call.

"Hi! My name is Scarlet Copperfield. I live in your apartment building at 57 Sterling Street. Apartment number thirteen."

"Hi there. Yes, I know the place. How can I help you?"

Scarlet felt frantic. "It's just that my key no longer works in the lock. Did you, by chance, change it?"

"I did," the landlord said. "Owen Wellesley contacted me about a recent robbery and wanted all-new locks."

"Yeah! Owen. He's my boyfriend. He must not have remembered to give me the key?" Scarlet fumbled for words. "Do you have an extra? I could come by your office and pick it up."

The landlord's tone grew icy. "I'm sorry, but there is only one name on the lease. That's Owen's."

"But we've met before," Scarlet said. "About a year ago, I let you in to check on the radiator. Don't you remember? I've lived there for almost two years."

"Listen, I can't keep up with every random person who lives in my apartments. Owen is the one on the lease, so he's the one who has the new keys. Is it a problem for you to reach out to your boyfriend?"

"It's just that he's out of town right now," Scarlet tried.

"Then I guess you'll have to wait. Have a great day, Ms. Copperfield." And with that, he hung up.

That evening, feeling purposeless and lost, Scarlet returned to her parents' apartment and found Greta hard at work on a four-course French meal. Nobody had used their apartment kitchen with such grace and artistry in many months, and the sight was rejuvenating. For a long time, Scarlet watched Greta work, as though she was a ballerina on the stage rather than an older woman wielding a very sharp knife.

"Your father just told Ivy and James about the move to Nantucket," Greta explained to Scarlet.

"Uh oh." Scarlet slid onto the stool next to the island and leaned on her elbows. "How did that go?"

"Better than expected. Your father had already spoken with the high school advisor to make a plan. Since Ivy is a senior and basically finished anyway, she can continue her classes online and come back to graduate here in the city at the end of May. James can easily take his credits into his sophomore year at Nantucket High School and has already talked about trying out for the baseball team. Your cousin, Danny, is a senior at Nantucket High, and I'm sure he'll be thrilled to take James under his wing."

"Wow. You're right. That is much better than expected." Scarlet was almost speechless.

"Ivy was thrilled," Greta continued. "She said she's tired of high school, anyway. And James said the high school here doesn't have a very good sports program."

"We don't really have the space here in the city," Scarlet explained.

"No. I would think not." Greta slid a pile of chopped vegetables into a piping-hot skillet. "In any case, I hope you'll find the time to spend with us on the island. Your boyfriend is welcome, too. By twenty-two, I had already met your grandfather. I know what it's like to fall in love. You just want to be with them all the time!"

After a terrible pause, Greta turned to find Scarlet in a heap on the countertop. Tears quivered down her cheek, and her chin wiggled as she tried to suppress her sobs.

"Oh, honey." Greta hurried around the counter and wrapped her arms around Scarlet. "What happened?"

Scarlet sniffed and tried to mop herself up. "I'm sorry. Really. I don't mean to be so upset."

"You don't have to apologize for having feelings, darling. They're the most natural thing in the world."

A sob escaped, but Scarlet snapped her hand over her mouth. She didn't want her mother to hear.

"Please, don't tell my dad. My boyfriend and I broke up. I'm mortified." She stuttered, feeling at a loss. Could she trust her grandmother with her secrets? "My dad hated him so much. But I loved him. I do love him. I really do."

How she hated how much she still loved him, even after what he'd done.

"Don't worry, honey. Your secret is safe with me." Greta wrapped Scarlet's hair into a ponytail, getting the curls out of her face. "Maybe Nantucket will be a welcome relief for you, too. Maybe you can find a way to start again."

# Chapter Thirteen

Catherine's surgery was scheduled for February 15th. Already, the date rushed toward the Copperfield family, making everyone panicked. Bernard and Greta remained at the house for the duration, helping tie up loose ends at James's school, celebrating with Ivy as she finished her final in-person class, and cooking, cleaning, and boosting morale. Quentin was completely indebted to them yet knew they wouldn't take any sort of payment. They were there to prove their love for him. They were there because Quentin was on the brink of collapse.

A few nights before Catherine's surgery, Quentin proposed that James and Ivy head to Nantucket with their grandparents so that Catherine and Quentin could prepare for the big day. This was met with initial protests. *"We can't just leave Mom,"* Ivy blared. *"She needs us."* But Catherine understood Quentin's reasoning. Although she hadn't had any chemotherapy for a while, her exhaustion had mixed with her fear of surgery, and she confessed she found it difficult to make conversation, let alone pretend she wasn't terrified.

With all three of her children gathered around her on the couch, Catherine told them how brave they all were and that soon, their family would be together again on Nantucket. Quentin listened intently, trying to believe her.

"If you and James get a head start on Nantucket, you can make sure everything is ready for us when we get there," Catherine said to Ivy as she tucked a curl behind her ear.

Off to the side, Scarlet spoke up. "I'm coming, too."

Quentin peered at his eldest curiously. He hadn't expected Scarlet to take such an active role in the move to Nantucket. Since Greta and Bernard's arrival, Scarlet had spent more and more time at the apartment, cooking with Greta, having intellectual discussions with her grandfather, and helping her siblings pack.

"Honey, you don't have to do that," Catherine said softly. "You have so much to care for here. And you've already gone above and beyond in the past few months."

But Scarlet raised her chin proudly and said, "I'm taking the semester off from NYU. I should have told you before."

Quentin's stomach dropped. He eyed Bernard, who nodded along with Scarlet.

"Dad? Did you know this?" Quentin asked.

Bernard hesitated, then replied, "She told us. I think it's a remarkable decision for a young woman to make. It's essential to recognize what you need at any given time. In fact, I think it's an important skill that many young adults never hone."

Rage spun in Quentin's chest. He wasn't sure what made him angrier: that Scarlet had dropped out of school or that she'd gone to his parents with the news rather than him. Then again, he couldn't make a big scene today in front of both of his other children and his ailing wife.

"It was the right choice, Dad." Scarlet spoke like a much older woman.

Catherine caught his eye after that. "Don't you remember

the choices you made as a young man, Quentin? Every single one of those choices led us here— to this beautiful apartment, these three kids, and your remarkable career. You had to trust your gut, didn't you?"

Although Quentin had plenty of responses to that, he knew it wasn't the time or place for an argument. "Very well," he said. "It makes me happy you'll be on Nantucket with your siblings. You look out for them, okay?"

"She always does," James piped up.

"And we'll join you as soon as I'm cleared by the doctor," Catherine said softly. "Soon, we'll be all together again."

That night, Greta and Scarlet cooked roasted chicken, roasted Brussels sprouts, and mashed potatoes. As Quentin entered the kitchen, he watched his eldest daughter remove an apple pie from the oven, announcing to her grandmother, "I think it turned out great." Quentin's heart ballooned with love for her. He'd wanted the world for her. *Why didn't she want the world for herself?*

Then again, she had been a tremendous help with her mother's illness. She was an adult that took care of herself, her rent, and her own responsibilities. Quentin gazed down at the perfect apple pie on the counter and blinked tears from his eyes.

"I'm so proud of you, Scarlet," he heard himself say.

Scarlet paused with the oven mitts still on her hands. She was incredulous. Finally, she said, "I really will go back to school."

"I know." Quentin shook his head. "But I hope you don't feel pressure from me. You have to do what's best for you."

Behind Scarlet, Greta continued to bustle around the kitchen, pretending not to listen.

"I'm proud of you, too," Scarlet said finally. Her voice broke.

Quentin laughed ironically. His mood was dark. "I don't know why you would be."

"Are you kidding? You're Quentin Copperfield. You're one of the most renowned journalists there ever was."

"You're parroting what other people say," Quentin said.

"Sure. But that doesn't make it any less true."

It had been a long time since Quentin had considered what his children actually thought of his career. He'd been so worried about what the rest of the world thought. Finally, he lifted his gaze to meet Scarlet's eye and said, "It means a lot to hear you say that. Really. Being at that desk was all I ever wanted."

"And you'll be back there in no time," Scarlet assured him, giving him a tender smile before continuing. "There's no doubt in my mind."

Greta took this opportunity to speak up. "That Jackson Crawford has heinous ratings. Just saying."

Scarlet laughed. "Grandma! You're such a gossip."

"It's not gossip if it's been written about in *The New York Times*," Greta returned, a sneaky smile playing at the corner of her lips.

That night, for the last time before Catherine's surgery, the entire family sat around the dining room table, joined hands, and prayed. Bernard thanked the heavens for the beautiful meal, for the communion as a family, and for the peace that awaited them in the next few months. When most of their hands broke, Quentin still kept Catherine's on his lap. Quentin could see her appetite was minimal and that the food on her plate would remain untouched. But she sat, rapt with attention, as her children and her in-laws swapped stories from their final day in the city, grateful for every interruption and every explosion of laughter. This was what family was all about.

* * *

Catherine and Quentin couldn't keep up with the photographs that came in over the next couple of days. Ivy sent pictures of a walk she, Scarlet, and James had taken on the beach with Alana, Ella, and their cousin, Danny— photos of the sunset, of the water as it cascaded along the sands, and of Scarlet doing handstands. Scarlet sent a video of how incredible Greta's kitchen was, along with another few photographs of the first meal she and Greta cooked together there. Ivy and Scarlet sent another photo of James standing outside of Nantucket High School with a pile of textbooks in his arms, along with one with his arm slung around Danny's shoulder.

"It's like a dream," Quentin said in the back of the car as they headed toward the hospital for Catherine's surgery. "I never imagined my children would know their aunts and cousins."

Catherine smiled serenely. "And look at them all, getting on like gangbusters."

"They miss you like crazy," Quentin said.

"They miss you, too."

"I don't know about that," Quentin joked. "I've always been the bad cop."

"But you look great in that police uniform," Catherine teased. As Quentin chuckled, she wet her lips and asked, "Did you notice Scarlet hardly left the Upper West Side over the past couple of weeks?"

"Yeah. I wasn't sure what to make of it, so I just didn't say anything about it."

"That's for the best," Catherine said.

"I'd hate to hope that Owen is out of the picture," Quentin said.

Catherine looked at him, laughing with only her eyes. Slowly, the car shifted against the curb outside the hospital, and the driver hurried around to open the door. It was time.

During Catherine's surgery, Quentin took a very long and

frantic walk around the neighborhood. He was careful to pull his winter hat over his eyes, as the worst thing he could imagine right then was being recognized by a fan. He couldn't pretend to be anything but really worried. He couldn't pretend to be anything but a husband and a father.

When he paused to catch his breath, his phone rang. It was Alana.

"Hey there, big brother."

"Hi." Quentin wasn't sure how to joke right then.

"She's in surgery?"

"Yep."

"And what are you doing with yourself?"

Quentin explained he was walking aimlessly.

"Isn't it too cold for that? You should go inside. Get yourself a hot coffee," Alana urged.

Quentin didn't have time for advice. "How are my kids doing?"

"James stayed home from school today," Alana explained. "And the three of them are in the library, keeping each other company. They're eager for your call."

"I'm eager to call them."

Alana was quiet. There was a rush of wind on her end, which made him imagine her on the beach in front of The Copperfield House.

"They're doing well here," Alana said. "I hate that I've never known them before now."

"I hate that, too."

"They sure love you a lot," Alana added.

"I don't know about that."

Alana laughed. "Trust me on this one. I never had children of my own, and I don't regret that. I really don't. I hate when people pity me about my lack of children, as though I'm somehow less of a person because of it. But you did choose to have children, and you did choose to raise them right. So much so that they're older now, and they still love you. That's a victory."

Quentin's heart lifted. Alana's call was the single thing he'd needed to get him through this horrific afternoon. "Thank you, sis."

"Just get here soon, okay? We all need you, too."

"I will."

* * *

Quentin was allowed into Catherine's recovery room not long after she woke up. Bleary from medicine and anesthesia, she smiled at him joyously and wrapped her hand around his. Quentin was so overwhelmed by her smile. He realized that with his terror around her surgery, he'd never thought he would see it again.

"How many years have passed since I went under?" Catherine asked.

"The year is 2088," Quentin said. "And we've colonized Mars."

"Oh, dear. How is it?"

"Everything is basically the same," Quentin explained. "Except that there's no more pasta."

Catherine's face was stricken. "No pasta? Then there's no point to life at all!"

Quentin laughed a little too long and swept away his tears. "I love you."

"I love you, too. But don't joke about pasta like that."

"I never will again."

Miraculously, the doctor cleared Catherine to go to Nantucket Island ten days later. There wasn't much to prepare for, which seemed to go against the basics of what it meant to move states. Quentin packed their suitcases and then hired one of his neighbors to check on their apartment and water their plants. He even checked in at the station to tell the producer where he was off to. And by February 27th, he and Catherine were in the back of the car, speeding toward Nantucket, their hearts full of expectation. No, they didn't yet know if she was clear of cancer. That news would come later. But something about the surgery, the change of scenery, and the reunion with their children made them endlessly optimistic.

"I can't remember the last time I left the city," Catherine said as she gazed out the window. For the first time in ages, she'd put on makeup, and the effect was startling and beautiful.

"It's weird not to be surrounded by massive buildings and endless smog," Quentin joked.

"And it'll be so quiet on the island," Catherine breathed. "I remember when I first met you, I couldn't wait for you to take me to Nantucket and teach me to sail."

"I'm sorry I never did that," Quentin said.

"You are now, dummy."

Quentin laughed. "I take it you have plans to spend all summer there."

"Maybe into the autumn, too." Catherine's eyes glittered.

It had been a long time since they'd discussed the future. Talking about the future had felt too frightening, as they'd become aware that the future wasn't a guarantee.

They were quiet for a little while, both stewing in their thoughts. Since the surgery, they'd spent so much quality time together without their children around, much more than they had in years. They'd played games, watched movies, told each other stories of the past, and discussed their hopes and worries about their children. The idea of becoming "empty-nesters" thrilled them, although it terrified them, too. *What would they do without James and Ivy around? What would they worry about?*

Suddenly, Catherine spoke.

"How are you feeling about the show?"

In all their time together over the past ten days, neither of them had discussed the news station. It had been like a very long game of Taboo.

"Oh, gosh. I miss it." Quentin surprised himself with a simple answer.

"I know you do." Catherine squeezed his hand.

"But I'm learning to figure out who I am without it," Quentin continued. "And I've thought so much about all the time I've missed with my family."

"We missed you, too."

"I don't know if it was worth it," Quentin said.

"You can't regret that time, now." She paused, searching for the right words. "And if you want to go back to your news desk, I know they'd take you."

When their driver parked them in the belly of the ferry, Quentin and Catherine got out of the car to stretch their legs. Out on the top deck, Atlantic winds tore through their hair. Quentin bought them both hot chocolates and wrapped one arm around Catherine's thin frame. "Tell me the minute you get too cold."

Catherine nodded and sipped her hot chocolate. She looked euphoric. Above them, the ferry horn blared, and the sound rushed out across the Nantucket Sound.

"How did I get so lucky to have such a great love?" Quentin said suddenly.

Catherine lifted up on her toes and kissed him. Quentin's heart surged with love. Why had he been allowed such magic? People searched their whole lives for such joy.

# Chapter Fourteen

Scarlet's first two weeks at The Copperfield House had been nothing short of miraculous. Nearly every day, she pinched herself as a reminder that she'd done it. She'd successfully run away from her problems. Owen was miles and miles away— and she was safe from his manipulation. She was safe from the city that had chewed her up and spat her out. She was in the warmth of The Copperfield House, together with her aunts, cousins, and grandparents who loved her. Beyond that, her mother's surgery already seemed like a tentative success— and she was so ready to start fresh on the island.

Then again, it was terrible to keep what Owen had done a secret. On Scarlet's darker nights, she remembered the truth. He'd stolen from her. He'd lied to her. Probably, he'd never loved her at all and had just used her for her father's name and wealth. When she'd called the police to discuss the matter, the police explained they'd spoken to the current tenant and learned that the insurance had been paid out. Scarlet had tried to explain. "My ex-boyfriend stole from me. Because the insurance was in his name to begin with, he got all the money. I don't know what to do or where to turn." The policeman had suggested Scarlet was stupid not to put the lease or the insurance in her name. She hadn't bothered to use her father's name. It would have only complicated things.

Because Scarlet didn't have many belongings after Owen had changed the locks, she used some of the cash she still had from her waitressing job to go shopping with Ivy. After all, she could only wear the sweatpants, sweatshirts, one pair of jeans, and a few t-shirts she'd brought from New York. If she really planned to spend the duration of spring at The Copperfield House, she wanted to look and feel her best.

"Why didn't you pack more stuff?" Ivy asked as she waited outside the dressing room.

"I just can't get to it right now," Scarlet answered honestly.

"What do you mean? Did something happen with Owen?"

Scarlet pulled open the curtain and glared at her sister. "I don't want to talk about it. What do you think of these jeans?"

Ivy put her hands on her hips. Scarlet's little sister was too smart for her own good. "Why don't you just tell me? It's not like you to not see Owen for this long. Heck, it's not like you to not bring him up every other sentence."

Scarlet rolled her eyes and jumped back into the dressing room. "We broke up. Obviously."

"Oh, Scar." Ivy sounded genuinely concerned. "What happened?"

Scarlet grumbled. "We just grew apart. You'll know what that's like when you're older."

Now, Quentin and Catherine were already on the ferry, and The Copperfield House was vibrant and almost ready for their arrival. Scarlet, Ivy, and James had decorated the bedroom their parents would share with flowers and a hanging sign that read: WELCOME HOME, MOM. Greta and Ella bustled around the kitchen to prepare the last of the welcoming feast, and James and Danny tossed a football in the living room, narrowly missing a few family heirlooms.

Meanwhile, Scarlet, Alana, Ivy, and Julia were in the artist residency, reading over a play Greta had recently written. Scarlet and Ivy had fallen in love with Alana's acting school and begged her to read lines with them all the time, which had brought them all closer.

"Come on, Scarlet. Really put your heart into this scene," Alana urged her.

Scarlet cleared her throat. "I can't believe you. You left me here in the darkness, nursing your baby, while you ran out into the chaos of the night. No wonder women never become what they're meant to become. We've got it all— the brains, the beauty, the motivation. But we have empathy, too. And that same empathy keeps us home alone at night while you run after your dreams."

"Yes!" Julia clapped her hands and nudged Alana, who nodded intently.

"That was fantastic, Scarlet. You really channeled your anger." Alana smiled at her.

To Scarlet, Alana was a beauty queen in the truest sense. She was light on her feet, had perfect posture, always knew what to say, and styled her hair and makeup with expert precision every single day. In fact, Scarlet hadn't yet seen her aunt in a pair of pajamas, despite them living in the same house for two weeks. It was as though she thought she was on the verge of being discovered, even though she'd already had her modeling and acting career. Scarlet supposed that kind of thinking just never really went away.

By contrast, Julia was a bit more like Scarlet's mother. She was rougher around the edges and quick with a laugh, and her hair was often frizzy and wild around her ears. This was the woman who'd once been married to Jackson Crawford, the terrible man who'd taken over Quentin's desk. It was hard to put those pieces together.

Julia's current boyfriend, Charlie, couldn't have been more perfect for her. He often surprised her with flowers, lifted her into his kisses, and complimented her hair even on its most chaotic days. When Ivy had learned of Charlie and Julia's high school origins, she'd practically swooned. "I never met the love of my life in high school," she'd complained.

"Grandma really knocked this script out of the park," Scarlet said, studying the last of her monologue.

"I think we should definitely perform it toward the beginning of summer," Alana explained. "We'll have auditions, of course. But I imagine you're a shoo-in for this part."

"Just give the girl the part, Alana," Julia said.

"Ivy? Are you interested in having a role?" Alana asked, studying the younger Copperfield intensely.

Ivy nodded. "Yes, I would love that."

"Whoo-hoo. I think Quentin and Catherine are here!" Ella's voice rang through the halls of the Copperfield residency.

Scarlet and Ivy abandoned the play altogether, leaping toward the hallway, with Julia and Alana hurrying behind them. They bolted through the door that separated the artist residency from the family house and were immediately blasted with crisp, cold air. In his excitement to see his parents again, James had rushed through the front door and left it wide open.

As Scarlet and Ivy ran onto the porch, their father helped their mother from the back of the car. James waited until their mother was stable and then wrapped his arms around her, careful not to touch her wounds from the surgery. The sight of her little brother hugging their mother like that nearly destroyed Scarlet. Their mother's eyes closed as she traced her fingers through James's hair.

"Mom!" Ivy shuffled up behind James, and Scarlet followed after her.

Catherine opened her eyes again and smiled at her daughters, then pressed her hand over their cheeks. Beside her, Quentin raised his chin to take in the sight of the house he'd grown up in. Scarlet turned to follow his gaze, considering the weight of the moment. When Quentin was eighteen, he'd probably never imagined himself moving his family into his childhood home.

"What an extraordinary place," Catherine whispered, just loud enough for only her children and husband to hear. She turned her head to kiss Quentin as the other Copperfields bustled out of the front door.

"Aren't you a sight for sore eyes!" Greta paused in the doorway and waved.

Ella, her husband Will, Julia, Alana, and Danny walked tentatively down the front step, careful not to interrupt the family reunion too soon.

"Let's get you out of the cold." Quentin gripped Scarlet's mother's elbow and guided her toward his family, who greeted her warmly.

"I can't believe you're finally here!" Julia said.

"Your children have decorated your bedroom for you," Alana chimed in.

"Goodness! I could hardly get them to clean their bedrooms back at home," Catherine joked.

With Quentin's help, Catherine took the porch steps slowly. Scarlet walked behind her, watching her mother like a hawk. If she stumbled, Scarlet was prepared to lurch forward and catch her.

The first room of The Copperfield House was the main gathering area for the family, complete with cozy couches, bookshelves, a crackling fireplace, and a baby grand piano, which Bernard often played deep into the night. The twinkling of his playing was the last thing Scarlet often heard before she drifted off to sleep. When Scarlet had asked Bernard why he liked to play so late at night, he'd said it was a way to keep his nightly fears at bay. Scarlet hadn't asked him what fears he had. All humans lived with their own private anxieties and fears. Now that she was an adult, she understood that all too well.

Scarlet's mother and father sat on the couch near the fireplace. Catherine smiled nervously at everyone, exhausted from the trip. Greta rushed in and out of the kitchen, offering drinks and snacks. As usual, since the diagnosis, Catherine didn't have much of an appetite. This worried Scarlet. A childish part of her had expected Catherine to be completely healed now that the surgery was over.

"This place is so magical, Greta," Catherine complimented as she finally agreed to eat one-half of a croissant. "No wonder it has a name. 'The Copperfield House.' It's one of those places that has its own personality."

Greta smiled broadly. "We bought it when it was falling apart. Day after day, Bernard and I put it back together again. We painted and sanded and wallpaper-ed and tile-d. Goodness, I thought it would take forever."

"They were still working on it when I was a kid," Quentin said.

"We put him to work as soon as possible," Greta said with a wink. "Now, where is that father of yours? He should be down here." She scrambled for the staircase to fetch him from his study.

Scarlet had already grown accustomed to this schedule. Greta was more of a morning writer. She woke before the sun, wrote, and edited her short stories and plays, made breakfast for whoever was around and hungry, and then worked another few hours till lunch. By contrast, Bernard liked to work in the evening as the sun waned over the water. When he was finished, he and Greta normally sat on the enclosed porch and listened to the waves as they washed against the shore.

This sort of love captivated Scarlet. Then again, Danny had told her that Greta and Bernard had only just gotten back together again. For nearly twenty-six years, they'd been more or less separated. Danny had put it like this: *"All we know is, one day, Grandma ran off to Paris. Grandpa chased after her, brought her home, and kissed her next to the Christmas tree. The rest is history, I guess."* Danny had shrugged at the simplicity and then gone on to explain that his parents, Ella and Will, had also almost gotten divorced. It was a complicated family— one that suited Scarlet.

Not long after Bernard raced downstairs to say hello, Catherine confessed she needed rest. Quentin helped her to her feet as she thanked everyone for the warm welcome. Greta assured her there would be plenty of food left over if she wanted to make herself a plate later. Alana then joked there was "always enough food at The Copperfield House." Everyone agreed.

Scarlet, Ivy, and James followed their parents to the bedroom they'd picked out for them. They watched happily as Catherine made a big deal about their decorations, complimenting their flair for artistry.

"And have you three really been happy here?" Catherine asked, her face stoic as she studied each of them. "Because if you haven't been, we can turn around tomorrow and go back to Manhattan."

"Oh. I love it here!" Ivy was the first to answer.

"She's just happy she doesn't have to go to school anymore," James quipped.

Catherine chuckled and shifted under the covers. "And you, James? How is high school?"

"It's funny. It's sort of like going to a high school on television. There are jocks, cheerleaders, music nerds, science nerds, and everyone in between," James explained.

"And you like that?" Ivy asked doubtfully.

"I love it!"

"What are you?" Ivy arched her eyebrow.

"I haven't decided yet," James answered.

"And there's no rush to decide," Catherine assured him. "Really, you should be a combination of those things. Don't you think, Quentin?"

"Absolutely." Quentin sat on the bed next to their mother and tucked her gently beneath the comforter. He locked eyes with Scarlet as he added, "There's so much time to figure all that out."

One after another, the Copperfield children kissed their mother's cheek and returned downstairs. Quentin came like a shadow after them, exhausted but brimming with happiness. In the staircase, Scarlet turned to say, "She looks good. She has more color to her than before."

"She's been a little bit better every day," Quentin assured her. "Now, all we have to do is keep our spirits up. This sea air is already extraordinary, isn't it? I feel like I can breathe again."

Scarlet knew exactly what he meant.

# Chapter Fifteen

Catherine was often tired. She spent many hours in the bedroom she shared with Quentin, either propped up on their pillows or in the cushioned chair by the window, reading or watching television or gazing out the window. There was something so beautiful about her at the window as the early March light played across her features. Often, if Quentin came up to bring her a snack or a glass of water, he was so captivated by her that he had to sit across from her in the corner if only to capture the moment. It was yet another in a series of moments he hadn't imagined they would ever have.

Four days after Quentin's arrival to Nantucket, he just happened to catch James in the kitchen before school. The scene was incredible. Greta slid eggs and buttered toast onto James's plate, asked him about the paper he had due in a few days, and even teased him about a girl. Quentin had never heard this girl's name before. His son had a life Quentin didn't know anything about.

"Why don't I walk you to school?" Quentin asked James.

James cocked his head with surprise. In truth, Quentin hadn't had much time for James's activities for most of his life, and this question probably felt out of left field. A part of Quentin was terrified James would say no. But instead, he took a large bite of toast, shrugged, and said, "Sure, why not?"

"You need some fuel, too." Another round of toast popped out, and Greta slid a buttered and jam slice onto a fresh plate for Quentin. She'd used raspberry jam, his favorite.

"Do you ever forget anything?" Quentin asked his mother.

"I wish," Greta joked.

Quentin and James donned winter jackets but left them unzipped in the fifty-degree weather. This warm spell was not unheard of in Nantucket, but they would probably pay for it with another drop in temperature and snowfall before spring officially came.

"Is it weird to go to my high school?" Quentin asked because he was terrified that they would walk to school in silence.

"Naw. It's kind of cool. I found your picture hanging outside the gym."

The image of Quentin's basketball photograph flashed in his mind. "I can't believe they still have that hanging up there."

"My gym teacher says you were really good." James sounded boastful, as though Quentin's athletic abilities were much more impressive than his nightly news career.

"You mean Coach Hackley still works at the school?" Quentin asked.

"Yeah. He's not that much older than you, I guess."

Quentin's cheeks burned. When he'd been eighteen, Coach Hackley had had to have been in his thirties or forties. *Right?* Or had Quentin just been too young to understand that his teachers weren't that much older than him. Perhaps they'd just crossed the threshold into "adulthood" while he'd still had a couple of years to figure things out.

At Nantucket High, Quentin wished his son good luck and watched as he joined the steady stream of students. They all looked so young. Laughter was a cacophony over them, bouncing off the enormous trees that surrounded the school. They were the same trees Quentin had known, but about thirty years bigger.

That reminded Quentin of something. He cut around the corner from the school toward a little park. During his senior year, a goody-two-shoes student named Betty had arranged for them to plant a tree in their honor. The tree had been just a single stick with a few leaves hanging off it. Quentin had joked with a buddy that it wouldn't live through the summer.

It didn't take Quentin long to find the tree. It now stood twenty feet tall, perhaps more, and its branches were thick and twisted, competing against each other to reach the sun. Not sure what else to do, Quentin used the camera on his phone to take a photograph. He soon remembered he hadn't kept up with anyone from high school. Who could he send the photograph to?

Quentin got back home around the time Julia hustled back from her beach run. She wore a light jacket and a pair of black leggings, and she flipped her ponytail around as she gasped, "Dang it. When am I going to learn not to have that extra glass of wine with Alana at night?"

Quentin knew his sisters were close. He could usually hear them up a bit later than the rest of the house, gossiping in the enclosed porch or in the residency library. Their closeness had happened quickly, a result of them coming together to fight for their father's innocence. Although Quentin had helped with that video at the premier that had ruined Marcia Conrad's career, he hadn't exactly felt welcomed back into the fold. Besides. Almost immediately after that, Catherine had been diagnosed with cancer, and his life had flipped upside down.

"I should be like you," Julia said as they went up the porch steps. "It seems like you have a good sleep schedule."

Quentin cocked his eyebrow. "Man. I can't believe my little sister just called me lame."

Julia gasped with surprised laughter. "Lame? No. Healthy? Yes. Besides, you've been through so much. I don't blame you for getting some extra shut-eye."

Quentin opened the door, no longer surprised that they kept it unlocked. That was just the way Nantucket islanders did things. "It's been a long time since I had any fun. Maybe I'm too old for it."

"Are you kidding me?"

In the living room, Quentin turned to find his sister with her hands on her hips. "What? Maybe the time for fun is over. I have to make peace with it."

"I just can't accept that for an answer," Julia shot back. "Sleep schedule? Yes. No more fun? Ever? Absolutely not."

"What's going on out there?" Catherine's voice was like a song coming from the kitchen.

Quentin walked toward it with Julia hot on his heels. Surprisingly, Catherine had made it to the kitchen and sat with Ivy, Scarlet, and Greta, sipping tea.

"Hi, Daddy!" Ivy called.

Scarlet smiled at him but didn't speak.

"Did you just say the time for fun is over?" Catherine demanded. Her eyes spun with anger and curiosity.

"Cath, it's not like that. I'm so happy with our life." Quentin palmed his neck.

Catherine grimaced. "Oh, Julia. Don't even get me started. The man in front of you hasn't gone to a non-work-related party in, like, twenty years."

"Are you really selling me out like that?" Quentin laughed.

"It's true, Daddy!" Ivy cried.

"My own wife and daughter are sending me up the river," Quentin said.

"Wait. Only work-related parties?" Julia asked. "You haven't celebrated anything with friends?"

"I worked with my friends!" Quentin tried.

"You mean the people who kicked you out and replaced you with my idiot ex-husband?" Julia demanded.

Quentin grimaced. He sauntered toward the coffee pot, poured himself a half-cup, and turned back to face his family. To make matters worse, both Alana and Ella had heard the commotion and appeared behind Julia in the doorway. Like always, they were nosy sisters through and through.

"What's this we're hearing about Quentin being lame?" Ella asked.

"Ella. Come on. We can't all be celebrated indie rock stars," Quentin said. "Or top models. Or really cool owners of publishing companies."

Julia, Ella, and Alana's jaws dropped. It was as though they'd only just realized how much their brother respected them.

"That's it," Julia said. "We're going out tonight."

"That's what I like to hear," Alana said, clapping her hands together.

Quentin turned back toward his wife and made a face. But even she wouldn't hear of his retreat.

"You should go! I sleep half the day away, anyway. Besides. When was the last time you went out with just your sisters?"

The truth was, Quentin had barely ever been out with just his sisters. Maybe they'd grabbed a glass of wine or two during the previous year as they'd tried to work out the logistics of the "new normal" after Bernard had gotten out of prison. Quentin wasn't proud to remember that most of those wine conversations had turned into arguments. Could he act normally around his sisters? Could he show them how much he cared?

* * *

Quentin agreed to meet his sisters outside The Copperfield House at eight-thirty. In the bedroom, he tried on three button-down shirts before Catherine booted him, saying, "You're going out with your sisters, not on a date. You don't need to impress anyone."

Quentin kissed his wife goodbye and took the steps downstairs two at a time. Already, his three sisters waited in the cold, laughing together beneath the moon. They were beautiful together, three brunettes with similar smiles. It still boggled his mind to remember Ella wasn't genetically related to any of them. He hoped she didn't think of it at all.

"It's weird to walk to a bar again," Quentin said as he stepped in stride with his sisters.

"Don't you live in Manhattan?" Ella asked. "One of the most walkable boroughs in one of the most walkable cities in the world?"

"He's Quentin Copperfield," Alana reminded Ella teasingly. "He can't just walk anywhere. He'd get recognized."

"That would stress me out," Ella said. "I'm glad my band was only ever moderately famous."

"Didn't you used to get recognized?" Julia asked.

"When I was in my twenties, sure. But now that I'm in my forties, it's like the train has left the station," Ella said.

"You look fantastic," Alana pointed out.

"Sure. I know that. But I also know the realities of being in my forties," Ella said with a shrug.

Quentin was quiet for a little while, listening to the easy rhythm of his sisters' conversation. Gosh, it was like they could talk for hours. As he was decidedly not a woman in his forties, he wasn't sure how to relate to them. His skincare regime was not as elaborate as theirs. He liked to watch sports. His idea of a good time was delivering the news.

Julia led them into a dark bar that played blues music. They grabbed a table in the corner as a bartender named Val sauntered over and asked if the ladies wanted their usual.

"She knows us too well." Alana wagged her eyebrows.

"And what about you, honey?" Val looked at Quentin.

"Um. A gin and tonic?"

"Coming right up," Val said.

When Val disappeared into the throng of bar revelers, Quentin heard himself speak. "This place is really something?" He wasn't sure why everything he said was coming out like a question.

"It is, isn't it? We love it here. We especially fell in love with it over the winter. It's got this cozy energy you just can't find in the city," Julia said.

Quentin understood what she meant. Every person in there was decidedly un-Manhattan-like. Although everyone on Nantucket had enough money to survive, the people in this bar weren't the upper-crust vacationers who came to the island only when the sun shone. They were the sons and daughters of fishermen and perhaps the great-great-great grandchildren of whalers. They had Nantucket blood— just like Quentin did. Did that make them more like him than anyone on the Upper West Side?

After Val returned with three glasses of wine and one gin and tonic, Quentin's sisters lifted their drinks over the tabletop to cheer one another.

"To being all together again," Alana announced.

"I'll cheers to that," Ella agreed.

Quentin smiled nervously and sipped his gin and tonic. The icy liquid chilled his tongue. In the corner, an older guy in a baseball hat typed a number into the jukebox, and Supertramp's "The Logical Song" began to play. Quentin hadn't heard the song since his high school days.

"Wasn't this one of Dad's favorites?" Quentin asked.

His sisters laughed and nodded.

"He loved singing in that high-pitched voice," Julia remembered. "Mom always kicked him out of the kitchen when it got out of control."

"She had a habit of kicking all of us out of the kitchen," Alana said. "I don't think she got a lot of peace and quiet back in the old days. Four kids and all those artists in residence? Mom didn't stand a chance."

"She seems really good right now," Quentin admitted, remembering last summer when he'd wanted to move their mother to New York City so he could watch out for her. "It's bizarre to see her and Dad so in love again."

"Right?" Ella shook her head. "They've been head-over-heels since they got back from Paris."

"It's like not a day has passed since the nineties," Alana said. Conspiratorially, she added, "You know, Mom took off to Paris to go to some guy's party. We found the invitation and showed it to Dad, and Dad freaked out and immediately chased after her."

"You're kidding. That's way too much drama for people in their seventies!" Quentin laughed.

"They didn't have any drama for twenty-five years," Julia said. "They're making up for lost time."

"I tried to tell them not to drop in on you like that," Alana said suddenly, her eyes in slits. "Mom freaked out when she saw Jackson at your news desk. She said she had to go to you. It was mother's intuition."

Quentin waved a hand. "They came at the best time. I was in the middle of a breakdown, I guess. Scarlet was left to pick up the pieces of our life, which wasn't fair to her at all."

"Wow." Ella nodded thoughtfully, then added, "It's just funny. When times got tough in our family, we all took off for separate corners of the earth. Scarlet took the opposite route. She doubled down on helping you."

"I guess that makes her a much better person than all of us," Alana agreed.

Quentin hadn't considered it from that angle. He sipped his gin and tonic, then heard himself say, "Scarlet has hardly spoken to me in two years."

His sisters exchanged glances.

"We sensed something was off," Julia admitted.

"What happened?" Ella asked.

Quentin stuttered. "I, um. I wasn't exactly nice about her boyfriend."

"Quentin!" His sisters said his name in unison.

"I know. I know. But I have a feeling they broke up. She hasn't mentioned his name in quite a while."

"That doesn't mean you've gained back her trust," Alana pointed out. "Besides, if they've broken up, she might be embarrassed to come to you about it. She's worried you'll say, 'I told you so.'"

"Really?"

"Wouldn't you feel the same way with Dad?" Julia asked.

Quentin dropped his shoulders. If there was one thing he remembered from his youth, it was that he'd always wanted— no, needed— his father's approval. When he hadn't gotten it, his heart had broken.

The Copperfield siblings ordered another round of drinks and paraded into new topics. Alana announced that The Copperfield House would reopen as an artist residency that summer, with many of the Copperfields helping out as teachers and advisors. Bernard was nervous but excited to boost another generation of dreamers into the wide world of artistic promise. Ella and Will planned to work together to hone musicians, while Julia and Bernard would focus on the writers. They were still on the hunt for a filmmaker and glanced at Quentin, who had, admittedly, taken several film classes back in college and spent the majority of his professional life on camera. But how could he help at the residency? He was needed back in Manhattan. Eventually. Wasn't he?

After the second drink, Alana bolted to her feet and said, "It's Thursday. They're open."

Ella and Julia rolled their eyes but couldn't suppress their smiles. Meanwhile, Quentin realized he hadn't known what day it was for weeks. *Thursday, huh?* Could have fooled him.

"Come on," Alana said, tugging at Quentin's arm. "We have to go. It's the only way to welcome you home properly."

Quentin saw there was no getting out of whatever this was. "Are you going to give me a hint?"

"That's no fun," Alana said.

They paid the bill and headed into the chilly night, walking two and two through downtown Nantucket. At every corner, Quentin was accosted with memories. Near the gazebo, he'd kissed his high school girlfriend goodbye. Along the water, he'd talked to his buddies about their dreams of becoming someone, anywhere but here.

Quentin walked alongside Alana as Julia and Ella scampered forward. "They'll always be our younger siblings, huh?" Alana teased.

"Some things never change," Quentin said, although he genuinely felt that everything changed all the time. After a pause, he asked, "Was it weird for you at first? When you got back?"

Alana's eyes bugged out. "It was the weirdest time of my life. Whatever you're feeling right now, it's normal. Just let us know if we can help you with the transition in any way."

Suddenly, Julia and Ella disappeared into a dive bar that shook with a very loud speaker system. Quentin followed Alana inside to discover that Thursday night was karaoke night, and apparently, his sisters tried to never miss it. Several people called their names, waving from dark corners. On a small stage, a middle-aged guy with a sailing hat on sang "If It Makes You Happy" by Sheryl Crowe. Quentin's ears rang.

A large binder was shoved against his chest. Quentin blinked into Ella's eyes as she said, "It goes like this. Pick a song from this book, tell the bartender what you want to sing, then go up there and show these good people what you've got."

"Sounds like a challenge," Quentin said.

Ella smirked. "We've seen you read the news. But do you have any real talent?"

"Harsh." Quentin laughed and flipped open the binder. Alana retreated to grab them a round of drinks as Julia rushed to the corner to say hello to her boyfriend, Charlie. Quentin waved to Charlie as well, reminding himself that Charlie was no longer his kid sister's high school boyfriend, but a forty-something widow with two children of his own. Life had had its way with everyone.

"So? What'll it be, Mr. Copperfield?" Alana returned with drinks and eyed the binder.

"I think I have to go with a classic," Quentin said. He turned the binder around and pointed at a song he and Alana had sung from the front seat of his convertible on endless summer days.

"'Dreams' by Fleetwood Mac? You really are nostalgic, aren't you? Just like the rest of us."

When Quentin was called to the stage, he held his gin and tonic in one hand and the microphone in his other. The crowd turned to him, listening as his voice initially wavered and then soared. If there was anything he knew, it was how to work a crowd. No, he couldn't master Stevie Nicks' gorgeous, raspy vocals, but he put his own flair on them in a way that made his sisters roar.

"You killed it, bro." Julia hugged him as he collapsed from the stage.

"You've been officially inducted back into the Copperfield clan," Alana agreed.

"Welcome home," Ella finished.

And for the first time in what felt like ages, Quentin allowed himself to experience pure joy. There was so much more to life than the news, than the Upper West Side, than his yearly paycheck and bonuses. He'd discovered it on the little island of Nantucket, in a dive bar with his sisters. Maybe he'd never needed anything else but this— with his little family safe in The Copperfield House, asleep.

## Chapter Sixteen

From the back porch of The Copperfield House, Quentin could make out the silhouettes of his three children and Danny and Laura, Ella's children, as they stretched their legs along the windy beach. Catherine sipped a mug of tea thoughtfully and placed her hand on his thigh. "They look like a postcard, don't they?"

Quentin turned and smiled at his wife. After more than a week at The Copperfield House, her cheeks had begun to fill, and the hollows that had lingered beneath her eyes for months had begun to lift. It was as though she'd aged backward ten years. *Was it the sea air? Greta's cooking? Or just the enormous amount of love that echoed through The Copperfield House?*

"James made the baseball team," Catherine said. "I caught him this morning with a baseball hat on, looking at himself in the mirror."

"Uh oh. We have a jock on our hands."

"James always had too much energy for the city," Catherine said. "Remember when we used to take him to Central Park?

He chased after the ducks and kept up with the athletic dogs and marathoners."

"He couldn't have been more than four at the time," Quentin remembered. He shifted back against his chair and took a long sip of his tea. "Are Ivy and Scarlet happy, you think?"

"As happy as young women can be."

"What does that mean?" Quentin asked.

"Life as a young woman can be very difficult. The world has so many opinions about you— about whether you should have children or be successful or lose weight or have opinions," Catherine said.

Quentin understood that. Heck, he'd covered enough stories during the #MeToo movement to understand the horrors that darkened so many promising young women's lives. It was just difficult for him to extend those stories to his own daughters. To him, they would always be young.

"Maybe we can keep them here at The Copperfield House forever," Quentin suggested. "We can keep them safe."

"And then what?" Catherine laughed. "They'll be fifty years old and resentful you kept them here like caged birds."

"I just wish we could extend this happy time a little bit longer," Quentin said wistfully.

Catherine squeezed his thigh. After another pause, she lifted her hand and unraveled the scarf from her head to show off her hair, which had begun to grow back tentatively. Although it itched terribly as it came out, Quentin knew the sight of it excited Catherine. She'd always adored having long hair.

Very soon, Scarlet and Ivy scampered up the back porch steps and greeted their parents. Their cheeks were tinged pink from the fresh, chilly air. Ivy headed inside to do a homework assignment while Scarlet paused for a moment and peered out across the water. Orange light flickered along the waves.

But suddenly, the reverie was broken.

"I have to go into the city for a few days," Scarlet announced.

Quentin turned to look at her. There was a harsh edge to her voice, one that told him not to ask any more questions. Catherine's grip on his thigh intensified.

"Why?" Quentin asked. "Isn't this paradise good enough for you?"

"I need to take care of a few things and see a couple of people," Scarlet tried to explain without giving a smidge of detail.

"Who are these people? What are these things?"

"I'm twenty-two, Dad. I don't have to tell you every single thing I do or every single person I see."

An old anger reignited in Quentin's chest. Before he could stop himself, he said, "I thought you were finished with that Owen guy."

Scarlet's eyes were hard. "I should be back in a few days." She then turned on her heel and stepped through the porch door. It slammed shut behind her.

"Quentin," Catherine breathed.

"I know. I know." Quentin bowed his head. Why couldn't he stop himself? "I'm sorry."

"I'm not the one you need to apologize to," Catherine said.

Quentin shifted back, prepared to head up to Scarlet's room immediately. But Catherine told him to hold back.

"Wait till she gets back from the city. She'll have cooled down by then."

Quentin knew his wife was right. If he didn't let things quiet, they were apt to explode. For the next hour or so, he sat listlessly, watching the waves. Before long, he heard his eldest daughter saying goodbye to Ivy and then Catherine, who'd gone inside to rest. The final slam of the front door told him she was off for the evening. She would take the last ferry to the mainland, where she would take a bus to the city. He'd done the same as a young man.

* * *

A little while after Scarlet left, Quentin donned his winter coat and headed into the last light. Thoughtful, he wandered the streets with his hands in his pockets and practiced having a real, adult, and compassionate conversation with Scarlet. Although it was only in his head, he found it difficult to think of the right things to say.

Near the library, Quentin heard his name. He paused, turned toward the sound, and watched as a middle-aged man with sandy-blonde hair approached with the gait of a teenager. When he got close enough, his eager smile took Quentin all the way back to his high school days.

"Kenny Lager!" Quentin could hardly believe it. Spontaneously, he wrapped his arms around his old friend and hugged him.

"Quentin Copperfield, as I live and breathe." Kenny stepped back and assessed him. "You look a lot smaller in real life than on television."

"Are you saying the TV adds ten pounds?" Quentin joked.

"Naw, man. You look great." Kenny clapped him on the arm. "I heard a rumor you were around. My wife's sister saw you singing at karaoke night."

"Dang. This really is a small town, isn't it?"

"Did you forget?" Kenny laughed to reveal deep crow's feet and laugh lines around his eyes. As a teenager, he'd always been quick with a joke. Quentin was glad to see he'd spent his life like that. "You can't so much as sneeze around here without someone talking about it." Kenny's smile faltered for a moment as he added, "By the way, I heard about your wife. I'm sorry, man. I really am. How are you holding up?"

"Well, she had surgery. She's resting up now." Quentin felt tentative about talking about his wife's illness with a stranger. *But was Kenny a stranger?* "We won't know if the cancer is really gone for another few weeks, but we're hopeful."

Kenny nodded. "It's all you can be."

Quentin swallowed, suddenly anxious. He didn't know anything about Kenny. "Man, it's good to see you."

"You, too, man. You kind of took off there for twenty-plus years."

"Things got complicated there for a while," Quentin said.

"You're telling me. Man, everyone thought your dad was guilty! And I mean everyone. We're all eating our words now, though." He paused, then added, "You were always one of the best friends I had, Quentin. I should have reached out to you after your dad's sentencing."

"Naw. I was miles away in LA. I don't know how you could have found me."

"Hiding out, huh? I guess I would have done the same." Kenny laughed again, returning them to easiness.

"What are you up to these days?" Quentin asked. "Do you have children? A career?"

Kenny snapped his fingers. "I have kids, all right. Five of them!"

"Gosh. I can hardly keep up with three."

"They're a handful," Kenny agreed. "And I work at the whaling museum just down the road."

"Oh. Really? I always loved it there. Haven't been in years."

"Do you want to go right now?" Kenny asked.

Quentin stuttered. "Right now?"

Kenny dragged a set of keys from his pocket. "Come on. It's magical there after hours." Before Quentin could answer, Kenny turned on a heel and headed down the street, leaving Quentin to chase after him.

*Was this another reckless Nantucket adventure?* Maybe. But it was successful in that it made Quentin briefly forget his worries about Scarlet.

Kenny talked easily as they walked toward the museum, explaining that he'd worked there for twelve years by then and couldn't have loved his job more. He'd gotten a degree in museum studies and worked for a while at the Smithsonian in Washington D.C., but he and his wife had missed Nantucket too much to stay.

As they entered the museum, Kenny turned on the lights and led Quentin to the main hall, where a forty-six-foot sperm whale skeleton hung from the ceiling. Quentin lifted his chin and gazed at the enormous creature, imagining his ancestors and their five-year-long quests to hunt whales.

"Nantucket history is pretty long and in-depth," Kenny started to explain. "Our ancestors were just living out here in the chaos of Nantucket weather, without modern heating or cooling or protection. Big storms would come, both in winter and the end of summer, and our ancestors could do nothing but hide."

"Then again, the weather still has its way with us sometimes," Quentin said. "When it wants to."

"Right you are. Maybe our technological advancements aren't so powerful, after all." Kenny looked thoughtful.

Quentin walked slowly around the exhibits, inspecting old harpoons, blubber hooks, and other equipment their ancestors had used to kill whales and collect the "sperm" inside of them, which they later used to make oil for streetlamps in Paris and London and lighthouses along the coast.

Quentin, who'd spent decades of his life reading news that was fleeting, was fascinated with the density of this history. They were stories that lasted. They weren't immediately thrown out to make time for what came tomorrow.

Kenny showed Quentin his office, which featured a framed photograph of him, his wife, and their five children, who ranged from sixteen to five years old.

"You've got a teenager on your hands," Quentin said. "How's that going?"

"You know what? My son isn't such a bad egg. He tried out for the baseball team last week and made it."

Quentin's mood brightened even more. "You're kidding. My son joined the baseball team, too."

"You mean the Copperfield and Lager team extends to a second generation?" Kenny looked overjoyed. "Man, I can't wait to sit at baseball games with you. You wouldn't believe how cold it gets during those nighttime games."

Quentin's heart lifted. For years, he'd missed nearly every event his children had had. Now, he would be allowed blissful springtime evenings next to his old friend Kenny as their boys raced around the bases and celebrated a time-honored sport.

"Kenny, would you ever consider working on a documentary?" Quentin asked.

Kenny's smile dropped, but not in a bad way. It was as though he'd suddenly transitioned into "Museum Kenny" rather than "Friend Kenny."

"I've actually been a talking head on several history documentaries," Kenny explained. "I've always loved the idea of working on one of my own. Obviously, I'm drawn to the history of Nantucket."

"Same." Quentin hesitated. "For years, I've worked tirelessly at the news. Every story is temporary and immediately forgotten, which has made me crave something that lasted longer and more in-depth."

"Are you considering quitting the news for good?" Kenny's eyes widened. "My wife and I haven't taken a liking to that new fellow, Jackson Crawford." He shivered.

Quentin laughed. "Thanks for saying that. Really. But yeah, I don't know what my future holds. All I can do is listen to my gut, right? And right now, here at the museum, I'm remembering all these other versions of myself. I'm remembering that I don't have to be a prisoner to the nightly news for the rest of my working life. I can start brand new."

# Chapter Seventeen

After three weeks on Nantucket, Brooklyn was loud and chaotic, a bustling ecosystem of too many sights, sounds, and people. Scarlet walked into the corner coffee shop and weaved her way through the crowd at the register to get to Alyssa, who sat with a journal, a pen lifted.

"Hi!" Scarlet hated how nervous her voice sounded.

Alyssa turned, dropped her pen, and leaped up to hug Scarlet. "There you are! My island girl!"

"If only our islands were the same," Scarlet said.

"We're not so far from each other. We should meet in the middle of the ocean," Alyssa joked.

"On surfboards?"

"I can have my cousin, Cole, bring me by on the sailboat," Alyssa suggested. "We can pick you up and race around the Nantucket Sound."

"Sounds like a dream." Scarlet dropped into the seat across from Alyssa. After a late-night arrival to the city and a rough night of sleep, she felt despondent.

"So. You said you wanted to take care of this Owen issue," Alyssa said, her tone formal.

"Yeah. But now that I'm here, I'm exhausted by the prospect. I mean, everything was in his name. I have no proof that he stole from me."

"Have you tried reaching out to any more of his friends?" Alyssa asked.

"Yeah. Only a few of them answered, but they basically told me they didn't want to get involved with my 'relationship drama.' When I texted them that Owen had stolen from me, they blocked my number," Scarlet explained.

"Jeez. Loyalties run deep."

Scarlet dropped her face into her hands. Alyssa grabbed her wrist.

"Come on. Let's go to the police," Alyssa said.

"I already called them," Scarlet said. "They basically told me to leave them alone."

"But I'm here, now. They can't ignore two shrill twenty-somethings with nothing to lose," Alyssa said.

Not long after that, Scarlet and Alyssa mounted the steps outside the Brooklyn police station and waited on sticky plastic chairs for their names to be called. When they explained the matter to the woman at the front desk, she called in an officer who looked even younger than Alyssa and Scarlet. He chewed gum as he analyzed the case, then shook his head.

"You were the one who discovered the robbery," he said, pointing to the file. "But there's nothing to prove those items were yours."

"Come on. You have to understand. Her ex-boyfriend is taking advantage of her," Alyssa said.

"We get cases like this all the time," the officer explained timidly. "There's really nothing we can do unless you can prove that the items you claimed were stolen are still in some way owned by Mr. Wellesley."

"What do you mean?" Scarlet asked.

"Mr. Wellesley, your so-called ex-boyfriend, claimed insurance on the items listed here as stolen. If you were able to show Mr. Wellesley still owned these items after claiming them as stolen, we would reopen the case."

"And how in the heck are we supposed to prove that?" Alyssa demanded. "He blocked her. He's pretending she never walked the face of the earth."

The officer shrugged and looked back at the file. "People break up all the time. The fallouts look different every time. The last breakup I dealt with, the woman shot her boyfriend's ear off. When you compare the two, your situation looks a whole lot better."

Scarlet and Alyssa left the station and walked the streets of Brooklyn wordlessly. There was nowhere to go and nothing to do.

"I should probably just go back to Nantucket," Scarlet said.

"You should tell your dad what happened," Alyssa pointed out.

Scarlet stiffened. "You know what? I'd rather pretend it never happened than let him know how right he was about Owen."

"Your pride will destroy you one day," Alyssa said.

"Maybe it already has."

They walked a little while longer, looping through the Brooklyn neighborhoods they'd once held dear. Scarlet recognized some people from NYU, their backpacks bouncing on their backs as they traipsed to their next class. She spotted a woman she'd always run into at bars, one who'd always been a little too tipsy to remember having met Scarlet before. It was hard to believe that phase of Scarlet's life— the one when she'd lived with Owen, felt wanted, and happy was over.

And suddenly, out of nowhere, Owen appeared.

He walked perpendicular to Alyssa and Scarlet, his gait

confident. Scarlet stopped short and watched him as he walked around the corner and out of sight.

"What's wrong?" Alyssa asked.

Scarlet lifted a shaking finger. "I just saw him. Owen."

Alyssa's eyes widened. "You're kidding. We have to go after him!"

"What? No!" Scarlet was terrified. This was the man who'd robbed her and ghosted her. He'd not only broken her heart, but he'd blasted it to smithereens and taken her for all she was worth.

But Alyssa grabbed her hand and tugged her down the street, hunting for him. They lurched around the corner and then spotted him at the next corner, where he'd paused to look at his phone. Scarlet shrieked and ducked behind a street sign as Alyssa looked on.

"Oh my gosh. He's waiting for someone!" Alyssa hissed.

"Will you please hide?" Scarlet demanded.

"Is that the girl from Instagram?"

Scarlet peered around the street sign, lured by morbid curiosity. Sure enough, the blond and leggy woman Owen had met last summer stepped out of a coffee shop, lifted herself onto her toes, and kissed Owen on the lips. Allowing herself to see this was like an act of self-harm. As reality crashed around her, Scarlet bent her head with sorrow.

"Come on," Alyssa muttered. "They're moving."

"Alyssa, no. I don't want to."

But Alyssa was already after them. Scarlet groaned and hustled after her, frightened yet very interested. She felt like a ghost.

Blocks later, Scarlet realized where they were headed and stopped again. Sure enough, Owen and his girlfriend, Tiffany, turned to enter the apartment building where Scarlet and Owen had once lived together. They entered it just as Owen and Scarlet had entered it hundreds of times, hands clasped and happiness etched across their faces.

"They're living at your apartment!" Alyssa cried. "Can you believe this?"

Scarlet didn't want to. She rushed around the corner, out of sight, so that she could cry into her hands. The world was off its axis; it would soon roll through the solar system, away from the sun.

As Alyssa rounded the corner to console her, Scarlet's phone buzzed in her pocket. A part of her thought the call would come from Owen, saying he'd seen her stalking them. When her father's name popped up, relief flooded her. Scarlet answered it.

"Dad?"

"Hi, Scarlet. Thanks for answering." Her father sounded frazzled. "I mean, I know I don't deserve it."

Scarlet frowned. She hadn't heard anything so apologetic from her father, ever.

"Is everything okay?" Scarlet asked, thinking of her mother.

"Yeah. Everything's great." Quentin stuttered. "I just wanted to apologize to you about yesterday. Heck, I want to apologize for the past few years. It's been really hard for me to accept that you're getting older. Your mother tells me all the time how stubborn I am. I'm trying to overcome that."

Scarlet's eyes filled with tears. Beside her, Alyssa muttered, "Who is it?"

"I wanted to let you know that Owen is welcome any time," her father continued. "Maybe you should bring him by this week. I know your grandparents would love to meet someone you care about so much. And I would love to get to know him better. I owe you that."

Scarlet felt very quiet. She'd never heard her father like this before, and it both startled and exhilarated her. Did she want to lose this newfound respect with the truth?

"The thing is, Dad." Scarlet stumbled over her words. "I'm not as grown-up as I think I am."

"I know that, honey. Nobody is."

"No. Listen, Dad. Please. Just listen."

"Okay."

Quentin remained silent as Scarlet explained her situation. She started at the beginning, with Owen's supposed film project in Los Angeles, and ended five minutes ago, when she'd watched Owen and Tiffany go into her apartment. Throughout, Quentin was gracious enough to let her talk. And when he finally spoke, his voice was the one he used on the nightly news. It was grounded and trustworthy. It was eager to help.

"Scarlet? I'm going to pack a bag and come to Manhattan immediately."

Scarlet's shoulders loosened. "You don't have to do that."

"It's no trouble. I have a few things to take care of in the city, anyway. Meet me at the apartment tomorrow. We'll figure out a way through this. Together. Okay?"

Scarlet tried to keep the sob out of her voice. "Okay. Thank you, Dad. Really."

"No problem, pumpkin."

After they said their first "I love you" in many months, Scarlet and Quentin hung up. Scarlet pressed her phone against her chest and looked at Alyssa, genuinely shocked.

"Why didn't I tell him six weeks ago?" Scarlet asked.

Alyssa rolled her eyes. "Because you're stubborn. Duh." She then laced her arm through Scarlet's and directed them toward the street with her other arm in the air. "Let's take a cab back to Manhattan. I'm tired of Brooklyn, and I want something to eat."

In the back of the cab, Scarlet closed her eyes and listened to a staticky love song on the radio. Miles away, her father prepared to come to save her. She could feel him ranting and raving about Owen to her mother; she could feel the wide berth of his anger, which was all the more powerful due to his love for her, his first daughter.

# Chapter Eighteen

The Copperfield House was up in arms that night. Quentin wasn't able to keep the news of Owen's betrayal to himself. The fiery story exploded from his lips and affected every single person at the dinner table. Ivy burst into tears while James pounded his fist to the right of his plate. Alana forced Quentin to back up and start from the beginning to when they'd first met Owen. To this, Quentin cried, "I never liked him!" And Catherine said, "Oh, here we go."

"Wait. Did you like him?" Julia passed a bowl of green beans to Charlie but continued to look at Catherine expectantly.

"It's not that I thought he was the greatest person in the world," Catherine said. "But when your daughter comes to you and says she's found someone she really likes, you give him a chance. At least, I thought I should give him a chance at the time."

"And I thought he was a scoundrel from the start," Quentin said.

Greta smiled at Catherine. "He's never going to let you forget this victory, is he?"

"No way. He was right about Owen Wellesley, and now, he'll use this as proof he's right about everything for the rest of my life." Catherine laughed and scooped several garlicky sweet potato fries onto her plate.

Quentin's heart ballooned. There it was again: the expression, "the rest of my life." He now imagined him and Catherine in their eighties, their arms wrapped around one another as they walked down the beach. Her hair had grown in even more, with some curling into light wisps. Catherine had read that sometimes after chemo, hair grew back differently— curlier or in other colors.

"So, what's the plan?" Ella asked Quentin. "You're going to Manhattan tomorrow, and then what?"

"I would go to his apartment and tell him I know everything," Danny said with authority.

"Danny. You can't just go up to dangerous people and talk to them like that," Will said.

"I think I could take this film nerd," Danny shot back.

Everyone at the table chuckled.

"Poor Scarlet," Ivy mumbled. "She wanted to marry Owen! She told me."

"Thank goodness I didn't marry the first man I liked," Catherine said, eyeing Quentin mischievously.

"Who was that?" Alana asked. "And what would your life be like if you'd wound up with him?"

"Good question." Catherine nibbled the edge of her sweet potato fry. "I guess I'd live in a small town somewhere. My husband would be a history teacher."

"Noble profession," Bernard interjected.

"Of course!" Catherine agreed. "But every single day of my life would be planned and scheduled. There would be no more surprises. And although it's not always easy, my life as a

Copperfield has been wonderfully different. I've woken up every day to new opportunities and new stories."

Quentin's heart spilled over with love. He cupped Catherine's hand and lifted it to his lips.

"I just hope our Scarlet finds this kind of happiness one day," Catherine said. "She deserves it. And with this Owen, she's been through enough romantic heartache for one lifetime."

* * *

As Quentin packed his bags the next morning, Catherine walked him through the dos and don'ts of his arrival back to the city. "Remember. Don't say, 'I told you so.' She's waiting for you to say that, and when you do, she'll pounce on you."

Quentin zipped his suitcase and adjusted his winter hat over his ears. "It'll take every ounce of strength I have not to, but I won't."

"That's my guy," Catherine said. "Remember to tell her you love her and that you want to help her fight for her rights. This way, you show you respect that this is her story, not yours. This happened to her. Not you."

"Although this probably happened to her because she's my daughter," Quentin pointed out.

"Don't you dare remind her of that."

"Okay." Quentin sighed and kissed Catherine first on the cheek, then on the lips. "If everything goes according to plan, Scarlet should be back home by tomorrow."

"And what about you?"

"I'll be in the city just a little bit longer to tie up loose ends," Quentin said.

"And you don't want to tell me what this genius plan is?"

"I don't want to jinx it. And I especially don't want you to tell me it's too rash," Quentin offered.

"I'm sure it is," Catherine said. "I'm sure I would tell you you're a madman for even trying it. Unfortunately, that brain of yours makes me love you even more."

Quentin's driver dropped him off at the Upper West Side apartment that afternoon at thirty past two. The doorman waved Quentin in, speaking quickly as he said, "Your daughter and her little friend seemed to have so much fun last night!"

Quentin paused and gave the doorman a harsh glance, which led the doorman to say, "A female friend, sir. I promise you that."

"Thank you," Quentin said, feeling foolish. "And thanks for watching out for them."

"My pleasure."

Upstairs, he found Scarlet at the kitchen island, reading a magazine. She had her hair up in a ponytail, and her eyes were blotchy from crying. When the elevator dinged, she rushed for him and hugged him, which reminded Quentin of hundreds of other hugs from a much younger Scarlet. He was her father. He'd come to save the day.

Neither of them had eaten lunch, and Quentin suggested they order in to discuss more of the specifics of Owen's con-artistry. True to form, they ordered far too many items from the Thai restaurant down the street and found themselves with too much food and not enough space in their stomachs.

"I think I ordered enough for our entire family. These are the spring rolls Ivy likes, and oh, your mother loves these dumplings," Quentin said.

"Mom is obsessed with them! Usually, when she's here, I have to grab one quickly before she eats all of them." Scarlet smiled and stabbed through some roasted vegetables with a fork. "How is Mom doing?"

"Every day, she gains a little more strength."

"The sea air has been good for her," Scarlet agreed.

"Your aunts have already taken to her, which means I have

to stay in line," Quentin continued. "As usual, the women in the Copperfield Family wield all the power."

"Come on. Alana, Julia, and Ella are thrilled you're there, too," Scarlet said. "They showed me so many videos of you that night at karaoke. They couldn't believe the 'great' Quentin Copperfield would embarrass himself like that."

Quentin winced. "Well, you do what you can to show family you care, I guess. Sometimes, that includes embarrassing yourself."

"I hope you invite me next time," Scarlet said eagerly. "I have to see this for myself."

Very soon, they switched to the topic of Owen. Quentin had come with an extensive list of questions to ensure he understood everything from Scarlet's point of view. He then asked for a list of the items Scarlet had cited as stolen in the police report, which Scarlet sent to him via text message.

"The police shoved me aside," Scarlet explained. "I've asked for their help twice."

Quentin nodded and licked his lips. It wasn't every day he got to orchestrate such a delicious plan. It reminded him of the old days of journalism when he'd been able to chase after a story and watch it mold and change before his eyes.

"So. What's the plan?" Scarlet asked. She slid the leftover Thai boxes into the fridge and smacked her hands together.

Quentin stood at the island and studied his daughter, terrified she would blow off the handle. "It would really be better if you head back to Nantucket while I deal with this."

For a split second, Scarlet's face crumpled.

"I need you to be patient with me," Quentin explained. "As you know, this is a very delicate situation. I hate that this happened to you. It never should have."

"I was just so naïve and stupid."

Quentin shook his head. "Listen to me. You weren't stupid, okay? Trusting someone you love doesn't make you stupid. You did your best with the information you had. Now, that information has changed, and we're going to use it."

Scarlet's jaw was stiff. "Why can't I help you?"

"Because we need the element of surprise," Quentin said. "And we can't have that if you're involved. He'll see you coming from a mile away."

Quentin didn't say the truer reason he wanted her gone. He wanted her between the safe walls of The Copperfield House and miles and miles away from Owen Wellesley. He wanted to give her the gift of peace.

After their chat, Scarlet retreated to her bedroom to call a friend. This left Quentin in the living room, his head a mess of unfinished thoughts. He dialed the number of his nightly news producer, the same one who'd told him Jackson Crawford was replacing him, and waited as the phone rang out across the city.

"Quentin Copperfield! Good to hear from you." The producer sounded pleased. Quentin assumed this had something to do with the public's dislike of Jackson.

"Hi there. How are things at the station?"

The producer grumbled. "I assume you've seen the ratings."

"I might have spotted them."

"Ugh. It's been a nightmare. On top of that, my assistant has reached out to your assistant twelve or thirteen times to see when you want to come back on the show. Your assistant keeps pushing back. Telling us you're taking personal time. But how much personal time does a man like Quentin Copperfield need?"

Quentin wanted to laugh but held it back. He couldn't sour his plan by ridiculing this producer.

"Listen. I can be on the show as early as tomorrow night," Quentin explained. "And I have an idea for a segment if you're up for it."

"The brilliant mind of Quentin Copperfield has a story. I'm all ears," the producer said.

Quentin wanted to tell the producer to stop licking his boots. Instead, he cleared his throat and began to articulate his idea. The producer didn't have to know the story itself was instrumental in taking down Owen Wellesley. Nobody did except Quentin himself.

# Chapter Nineteen

Quentin placed Scarlet's suitcase in the trunk of the car and leaned into the backseat to hug her goodbye. Although it was hours before he was slated to head back to the station, hours before he would begin the first steps of his plan, he was exhilarated. Here, in the bright light of the March morning, he said, "See you tomorrow, I hope," to his daughter, gave his driver the biggest tip around, and waved goodbye until the car turned the corner and disappeared from sight. Immediately, his smile fell, and his pulse quickened. He had to prepare.

To get his head on straight, Quentin went to the gym inside his building to lift weights and run on the treadmill. A television played daytime talk shows as he raced. Two women spoke about two different cutting boards and which one was more durable. Another guy showed off a spray that supposedly removed all kinds of stains from white t-shirts. Another couple tried out several different mattresses, bouncing on them, wearing gleeful smiles.

With each step on the treadmill, Quentin was overwhelmed with sadness. The people on these daytime talk shows and commercials had all wanted to be actors. Their career trajectories had stalled along the way and left them with spray bottles that promised magic stain removal. The would-be actors did what they could to survive.

Even Quentin had once wanted to be an actor. He'd fought valiantly, memorized lines, gone to endless auditions, and eventually found himself to be a little too old to play a high schooler and a little too young to play a sitcom dad. It had been disheartening, to say the least.

The news had been his sweet relief— and then it had become his everything.

Quentin showered, changed into slacks and a nice shirt, puffed himself with cologne, and swung his wrapped suit over his shoulder. Because his driver was almost to Nantucket by now, he hailed a cab to take him to the station. The driver was very excited about this and asked him twice if Quentin was going on-air that night. "We've missed you, my man. We need you to read the news!"

Quentin smiled easily and thanked the man. After he paid and stepped out of the cab, he stood in the splendor of the high-rise building that had been his kingdom for seventeen years. In some ways, it felt like returning home. In others, he felt like a ghost.

When the elevator dinged and he stepped onto the studio floor, PAs, interns, makeup artists, and producers smiled and waved hello, rushing around him as though he was a mountain, and they were little rivers and streams. Quentin questioned that for the first time. Had he frightened people with his power? If so, he resented himself for it.

As Quentin stepped toward one of the dressing rooms, he heard a familiar voice. It was Jackson's, and it was not happy.

"After everything I've done for this station. You're going to knock me down a peg like that? You're going to act like I deserve that?" Jackson demanded.

The producer spoke simply and without emotion. "As I said before, we are very grateful for your time at the front desk here at the nightly news. You've helped us through a very difficult time. But from here on out, Quentin Copperfield will be returning to his station."

"Great. The mighty King Copperfield has returned," Jackson blurted.

"I wouldn't take that tone with him," the producer warned. "He is very well-liked around here."

"Are you insinuating that I'm not very well-liked?"

"Quentin should be here any minute. He has a special report for you," the producer continued. "I assume you'll be up for it?"

"How can I say no to King Copperfield?" Jackson said.

"You know, you really could learn a lot from him. If you let yourself," the producer said. He then slipped out of the dressing room and walked in the opposite direction from Quentin, already muttering into his headpiece.

Quentin entered his own dressing room, had a drink of water, and eyed himself in the mirror. If he wasn't mistaken, the sea air had been good for him, too. The shadows around his eyes had lightened. He looked, if not five, then at least two years younger. He'd maybe lost a little weight, too— the healthy kind that made him look lither.

After he got up the nerve, he returned to the hallway to knock on Jackson's door. Jackson's abrasive "Come in" made Quentin grin. He adored making these sleazeball men crazy.

"Well, if it isn't Quentin Copperfield?" Jackson smiled his fake smile as Quentin stepped through the door. "I heard a little rumor you'd be back to grace us with your presence."

"Thank you for the warm welcome, Jackson. I've spent

some time on the seaside with my family. Can't recommend it enough."

Jackson blinked disdainfully.

"Anyway, I'll cut to the chase. I need a story to go on-air tonight."

"Tonight?"

"It's fast, but it has to happen. The producers have already contacted the interviewee to make sure he's available. And what luck! He is," Quentin said.

Jackson checked his watch. "It's three-thirty. You want this to be filmed and edited all before you go on at eight?"

"Sounds crazy, doesn't it? But I promise it will work." Quentin smiled, even though his heart pounded so loudly he thought he might pass out. He then dragged a piece of paper from his pocket, which he passed to Jackson. "I've already done all the research and come up with a list of relevant questions. Don't worry. The producers have cleared them."

Jackson's nostrils flared as he read through the list. He then lifted his eyes to glare at Quentin impatiently. "This is a puff piece."

"It's really not," Quentin countered.

Jackson coughed. "You want me to interview this up-and-coming artist about his life? What's the angle?"

"The angle has to do with the difficulties of affording a life-style as an up-and-coming artist in Brooklyn," Quentin said. "It has to do with the economy, with how the world regards artists, and how the young people in our city still fight for their dreams, despite not earning enough."

Jackson didn't believe him. Still, Quentin knew Jackson had to do anything he said. If he didn't, he would lose his position at the nightly news, even as a correspondent, and it was unlikely he would be wanted at another station, especially after his horrific ratings. He was trapped.

"And you can promise me my contract here at the station is

safe?" Jackson asked, disgruntled. "Despite the fact that you've decided, seemingly spontaneously, to return."

"Your contract is safe for another five years," Quentin said. "I'll go out of my way to make it so."

"You had better." Jackson continued to read the questions Quentin had written out. His cheeks were sour green.

A half-hour later, Jackson and the camera crew were prepped and ready for filming. Quentin tagged along in the nightly news van and bubbled with excitement and fear. It had been ages since he'd gone on location in the city, and he loved listening to the banter between the camera crew members and feeling a part of the inner mechanics of the station.

"Who is this guy you're interviewing?" one of the cameramen asked.

"Some young indie filmmaker," Jackson barked.

"He's an up-and-comer," Quentin explained.

"Apparently, Quentin has an eye for filmmaking now," Jackson said sarcastically.

"I believe in the artists of this city," Quentin said. The only pleasure he took in this was making fun of Jackson in plain sight. He deserved it after what he'd done to Julia.

The van parked directly outside of the apartment building in which Scarlet and Owen had lived together for two years. Those two years had been monstrous for Quentin, who'd just wanted to keep his little girl safe.

After the engine was turned off, Jackson and the crew got out and assembled in front of the building. Jackson had on his "news" face." Quentin hovered in front of the monitor inside the van and turned on all speakers to ensure he heard and saw everything that happened from the moment Jackson and the camera crew met Owen. He was breathless, to say the least. Two other sound guys stayed behind with him to make sure everything worked fluidly. Quentin thanked them for their commitment to the job, and they smiled with surprise. It was a rare thing that anyone noticed the hard work they did. Quentin cursed himself for not saying so more often.

"Oh. There he is." One of the sound guys pointed at the monitor as Owen Wellesley walked out of the front door of his building. He floated down the staircase easily, and his expensive trench coat whipped out behind him. The glasses were typical-Owen— hipster, thick, and of the moment. Under the trench, he wore a mustard-colored sweater and a pair of corduroys.

"He looks like a cartoon character," another sound guy joked.

"All these artist types have to cultivate their look," the other said.

On the monitor, Owen reached out to shake Jackson's hand. "Hey, man. Welcome to Brooklyn."

"Thank you. Do you mind if we get started right away? The cameras are already rolling."

Owen's face twitched so that he peered directly at the camera, beaming with pride and arrogance. You could see that he actually believed what the station had told him: that he was a good enough up-and-comer in the film industry to be featured on one of the most popular nightly news channels of all time. Last night, Quentin had checked Owen's credentials and discovered he'd done only five music videos and three short films— none of which had made a splash in the film or music industries. Owen was delusional. And he'd walked right into Quentin's trap.

When the producer had called, it was miraculous that Owen hadn't asked about Quentin's involvement in the station. This was more proof of Owen's ego. But it was also proof that the world had already begun to forget about him. He'd been off the air for many weeks at that point. It was the perfect time to step away for good.

"Let's do it," Owen said to Jackson. His confidence was electric.

"Great." Jackson turned to address the audience. "My name is Jackson Crawford, and I'm here this afternoon in Brooklyn with a man you probably don't know yet. Mark my words, folks. One day, you will.

"Introducing Owen Wellesley, an up-and-comer in the film industry. He lives here in Brooklyn in this very brownstone we're standing in front of, and he's agreed to meet with us today to discuss the state of the film industry in this city and whether or not it's logical or advisable to chase after your dreams in this economy. For the younger people at home, listen up. We might have a few answers for you about your future."

Owen's smile was wide and nervous.

"Owen, tell me. Do you live here alone?" Jackson turned and began to walk toward the brownstone, tilting his head so that Owen followed along.

"No. Living alone in 'this economy' is basically impossible," Owen joked. "I'm lucky. I get to live here with my beautiful girlfriend." He turned to stare into the camera as he added, "Her stage name is Tiffany Bunny. Watch out for her in the music industry, everyone. She's something special."

"That was a shameless plug," Jackson said. "You must really like her."

Owen nodded and hustled up the steps to let them into the lobby. The camera crew was diligent, tracing their every step as they walked up the staircase to the second-story apartment. Throughout, Jackson kept to the script Quentin had written him, which boosted Owen's ego every step of the way.

"Yeah. I mean, Brooklyn is the heart of the arts scene here in New York. But it's pretty rare to find someone with an actual voice, you know?"

"Explain what you mean, Owen," Jackson said.

"I mean, so many people are regurgitating the same stuff. I

know three filmmakers who made films about the same topic last year. And none of them had an interesting angle, either."

"So, you're suggesting that to be a successful filmmaker, you have to have something unique to show the world?" Jackson asked.

Owen nodded, his eyes wide. He reached into his pocket to procure his house keys, of which there was only one. Apparently, he'd had the extra security locks removed since he'd ghosted Scarlet.

"Where do you get these unique ideas?" Jackson asked as Owen slid the key into the lock.

"Dang. That's a hard question to ask a creative, you know? I mean, would you ask a bird how it learned to fly? It just does, right?" Owen pushed the door open and said, "Voila!" and smiled into the camera. "What was that old show from MTV? 'Welcome to my Crib!'"

Jackson looked at the camera with his fake smile. He then followed Owen into the apartment with his microphone lifted so that he caught more of Owen's monologue. As Owen talked about his fresh ideas for films and music videos and discussed how horrible everyone else's ideas were, the cameras set to work on showing off the apartment.

Quentin had only been to the apartment a handful of times. The camera showed the living room to be exactly the way he remembered it, complete with its massive flat-screen television and its gaming consoles. They didn't mean anything, though. Owen could have used the insurance money to purchase those things.

In the kitchen, however, things got juicier. *The china!* The china that had sat in the beautiful cabinet had belonged to Catherine's mother. Scarlet had reported it stolen, yet there it was, set up beautifully.

Just as Quentin had asked him to, Jackson commented on the antiques in the apartment.

"Oh, these plates?" Owen adjusted his hipster glasses. "They're family heirlooms. Babe?" He called through the house.

Suddenly, Tiffany Bunny appeared in all her blond glory. She smiled at the camera flirtatiously and clung to Owen's arm. "What's up, babe?"

"Tell these kind people who you inherited these plates from?"

"Aren't they gorgeous? They belonged to my grandmother," Tiffany explained. "I think it's so important for Owen and I to uphold the art of the past as we create art for the future. In one hundred years, I would hope people will still listen to my music and find a way to relate to it. You know?"

Jackson looked like he wanted to jump out the window. In the van, Quentin's hands were in fists. How he hated these men! How he hated that Tiffany lied to the camera about Catherine's mother's china!

"Mr. Copperfield? Are you okay?" One of the sound guys had noticed how strange he looked.

"Yes. I'm fine." Quentin smeared his sleeve over his sweating forehead.

On the monitor, Owen and Tiffany showed off the rest of the apartment, including Tiffany's gorgeous collection of jewelry. Just as Quentin had instructed, the camera panned over the necklaces, bracelets, and rings as a way "to highlight the trends of the current artistic age." There, hanging off to the right, was the locket Catherine had given Scarlet many years ago— the one that had held their photographs. Quentin could have cried.

Back in the living room, it was time for Jackson to wrap things up. Quentin had given him a doozy of a final question.

"So. It's clear to me and, I'm sure, the viewers at home that you live an artistic and fulfilling life, Owen," Jackson began.

"Now, it's time for us to discuss your current and future projects."

Owen began to stutter, trying to speak over Jackson. Jackson didn't let him.

"According to our sources, you just completed a six-week film project out in Los Angeles," Jackson said. "Can you tell us a little bit about that?"

Owen's facade fell away. Beside him, Tiffany lost her smile. They exchanged worried glances, searching for a way out of this.

"Oh. Yeah. Owen, you were in LA. For that film project." Tiffany jabbed him in the ribcage. "Remember?"

Jackson smiled. "You must be very busy if you've already forgotten a six-week film project."

But Owen had lost all his coloring. His hand stretched over the microphone in Jackson's hand as he said, in a harsh whisper, "Who sent you?"

Quentin guffawed. *Maybe this kid wasn't so stupid after all.*

"Babe, he's Jackson Crawford. He's been on TV every night for the past few weeks," Tiffany murmured.

Quentin's smile nearly broke his face as he watched Owen realize what he'd done. He began to stutter, to heave. Quentin scrambled for his cell phone and called the police, sounding breathless as he ordered them to his daughter's old apartment.

"I'm going to need to ask you to leave," Owen said to Jackson.

Jackson lifted both hands. "And I'm going to have to ask you to keep your hands off my equipment."

"Hey. Get the heck out of my house!" Owen cried. His tone was now like a child's.

"Babe! Stop acting crazy," Tiffany said.

"Tiff, don't you realize who he replaced?" Owen pounded the side of his head, and his glasses became askew.

Jackson turned toward the camera with his microphone

lifted to his mouth. His smile was serene, the sort that America could trust.

"And that's a wrap on our crash course into 'the artistic side of Brooklyn.' I'm Jackson Crawford. Back to you, Quentin."

After that, Jackson and the camera crew scrambled from Owen's apartment. Before they could even make it to the street, the police arrived and scrambled up the steps to meet Owen as he tried to make a run for it. From the back of the van, Quentin watched as the police pressed Owen against the wall. Tiffany screamed and cried beside him, her perfect face now blotchy.

As the camera crew watched from the safety of the nose of the van, Jackson yanked open the side door to peer up at Quentin.

"I don't know what just happened," Jackson said. "But if anyone should be arrested for being annoying, it's him."

Surprising himself, Quentin turned and hugged Jackson, overwhelmed with how well he'd done. Laughter made him shake.

"Okay. Okay." Jackson stepped away from Quentin and stared at him. "You're a crazy guy, aren't you?"

"Only when it comes to my family," Quentin affirmed.

They were quiet for a moment, listening to Owen as he screamed at the cops to unhand him.

"Do you think Anna, Henry, and Rachel will find a way to forgive me? One day?" Jackson spoke very softly.

As Quentin howled on, Quentin's heart bled out at the sincerity of Jackson's question. *Was it possible that Jackson lived with regret?*

"I think you're going to have to prove to them how much they matter to you," Quentin said. "But if you love them, they'll find a way to forgive you. I have to believe that."

# Chapter Twenty

Julia's children were at The Copperfield House for a visit. Anna was twenty-three and a resident of Seattle; Rachel was a sophomore at the University of Michigan; and Henry lived and went to school in Chicago, a city Scarlet had never been to, although she'd always wanted to go. As the Crawford children filled The Copperfield House, laughter bubbled from room to room, and Bernard rushed from his upstairs study to greet them with hugs and questions about their studies and what they'd read recently. Greta set to work on baking and cooking, as she always did.

Together, Julia's children, Quentin's children, and Ella's children sat around the porch table, drank soda and terrible beer, and listened to music. The Crawford children had been informed of Scarlet's "Owen" conundrum, and they were now just as nervous as the rest of them about what sort of plan Quentin had concocted. Nobody was sure how he would find a way to prove Owen's guilt.

"So, your dad never liked him?" Anna asked with a rueful smile.

"He hated him," Ivy explained before Scarlet could.

"Ugh. That's the worst!" Rachel said.

Scarlet wrinkled her nose. "I thought I would feel more complicated about it. But honestly, I'm just grateful to have my dad on my side right now. We spent the past two years at odds with each other."

James nodded furiously, grateful that Scarlet finally acknowledged the chaos she and Quentin's bickering had brought to the family.

"I won't let it get like that again," Scarlet promised her little brother. "It was terrible for me, too."

"Look at all these grandkids!" Greta appeared with a platter of cookies and a nervous smile. "I hope I'm not interrupting anything." She placed the platter in the center of the table and stepped back to watch as all eight grandkids selected a cookie and thanked her.

"These are delicious, Grandma," Danny said. His lips were caked with melted chocolate.

Greta returned to the kitchen to continue cooking dinner. Scarlet burrowed herself deeper under a thick knitted blanket and listened to the waves cascade along the beach.

"Can you imagine what it's like to suddenly have eight grandchildren?" Laura suggested. She'd come in from the city that morning, as she'd heard that all of her cousins would be there for the first time ever.

"This is like heaven for her," Henry said. "We eat everything in sight and ask for more."

"My dad told me she was a prominent scholar at the Sorbonne," Scarlet said.

The other grandchildren nodded stoically. They took their family's history very seriously.

"It's just hard to believe she was in this house the entire time," Scarlet continued. "We could have had such an epic childhood here."

Suddenly, Scarlet's phone buzzed. It was a text from Quentin, along with an attached video.

"It's my dad!" Scarlet announced. "He sent me a video."

Together, the Copperfield grandchildren gathered around Scarlet's phone and peered down at the screen. When Scarlet pressed play, Anna shrieked. "Wait, that's my dad!"

Scarlet paused the video to take in the image. In the first seconds, Jackson Crawford stood in front of the apartment building she'd shared with Owen as Owen stepped through the front door in corduroy pants and a very expensive trench coat. What was her father up to?

"Keep playing it!" Anna cried.

Scarlet did. And over the next few minutes, she and her cousins listened as Owen explained to Jackson what it was like to be the most creative man in the world, as the camera traced a path through the apartment.

"The television! The gaming console! My grandmother's china!" Scarlet's voice cracked with disbelief. "It's all there."

A split second later, Tiffany Bunny appeared on the screen. Ivy rubbed Scarlet's back, fearful of Scarlet's reaction. But seeing them together in her kitchen made Scarlet feel very little. Owen seemed like a stranger, and Tiffany was someone she would never know.

"I can't believe our dad agreed to do this," Rachel muttered.

"He's normally not so agreeable," Henry said. "And this is basically a puff piece."

"Your dad must have talked him into it," Anna said.

"He's still Quentin Copperfield," Scarlet breathed. "He still has a little bit of power left." Miraculously, he'd used that little bit of power to save her.

The footage went on to show the bedroom, along with the jewelry collection and Scarlet's vinyls. Jackson then asked

Owen about the supposed film project in Los Angeles, which set off Owen's alarm bells.

"Oh my gosh. His eyes changed," James whispered.

"He looks insane," Ivy agreed.

When the camera cut out, Scarlet's tongue was very dry, and she took a long sip from Henry's domestic beer. The cousins were quiet for a moment until Danny howled, "Dang! That was cool."

"Do you think they'll show it on the news tonight?" Anna demanded.

But Scarlet had no idea. In slow motion, she stood and hobbled back into The Copperfield House with her phone pressed against her ear. By the time Quentin answered, she was weeping.

"Honey. It's okay," Quentin said.

The sound of her father's voice brought her back to earth. "That was incredible, Dad. Really. You got proof. I can't believe he was dumb enough to let them shoot that footage."

"We did a pretty good job of buttering him up," Quentin returned.

"His ego was always so malleable. Gosh. Where were you during filming?"

"I was in the van outside," Quentin explained. "I watched everything from the monitors and called the police to the scene as soon as I was sure."

"The police?" Scarlet was breathless.

"Owen caught on to our game and tried to run from the scene. Although the police weren't sure what was going on yet, they don't take kindly to anyone running from the scene. They apprehended him and have both him and his girlfriend at the station for questioning," Quentin explained. "Obviously, the camera crew got everything on tape. Owen Wellesley will be famous very soon."

Scarlet could hardly believe it. "Thank you, Dad. Thank you for doing this. It was such a reckless, insane plan."

"It worked though, didn't it?"

"It really did." When Scarlet closed her eyes, tears rolled down her cheeks. "Are you coming back to Nantucket now?"

"I just have to do one more thing," Quentin explained. "Turn on the news tonight. Eight p.m. sharp."

"I wouldn't miss it for the world."

* * *

That night at seven, the Copperfields gathered around the dining room table for a big and boisterous dinner. Greta had made beef bourguignon with fresh bread and watched expectantly at the head of the table as her grandchildren, three of her children, and spouses and boyfriends ate heartily. Bernard sat on the opposite end of the table, in heavy conversation with Henry about his recent reread of *Moby Dick*, which Bernard called one of the most poetic novels of all time.

Beside Scarlet, Catherine smeared butter on her bread. Her cheeks were fuller than they'd been even a day before, and there was a light in her eyes, one that made Scarlet think she was only a second or two from telling a devastating joke.

"Your father sent me the video," Catherine explained, just loud enough for only Scarlet to hear.

"I can't believe how reckless he was," Scarlet said.

Catherine smiled. "Your father was always a risk-taker. It's part of the reason I fell in love with him."

"I thought you were more of the risk taker," Scarlet said, thinking of her mother's career in journalism when she'd fought valiantly to get to the root of any story.

Catherine thought for a moment, dunking her bread into the beef bourguignon. "It's hard for me to remember all the different versions of myself, I suppose."

"Maybe it's time to take risks again," Scarlet said. "Maybe it's time to go out there and chase after stories."

"Maybe. Or maybe it's time to sit still for a little while and enjoy the beautiful life I've been given," Catherine said. "Maybe it's time to watch the sunrise and sunset, to paint pictures, to sleep in, and to read novels I've never had time for. Maybe the chase isn't everything anymore. Not the way it used to be. Gosh, when Quentin and I were young, we wanted everything. We wanted the best apartment, the top careers, and the most children. But slowly, we've gotten older. We've learned what actually matters. And now, here on Nantucket, I think we've found a rhythm that really suits us."

Scarlet put her fork down and stared into her stew. For years, she'd been running toward her college degree and toward Owen as quickly as she could. Now, with no goals before her, she'd stopped running. It felt nice to slow down. She was relearning how to breathe.

"Life has a way of making a lot of decisions for you," Catherine continued softly. "And change happens both gradually and all at once."

Scarlet wasn't sure what to say. She was twenty-two years old and had no idea what was next. But before she could articulate how scary this was, Greta cried, "Oh, goodness. It's almost eight. We have to get to the living room, stat."

Bernard turned on the television and increased the volume. The Copperfields grabbed whatever seats they could, with many of the cousins sitting cross-legged on the rug. Scarlet remained standing with her arms crossed over her chest and her mind whirring.

Very soon, Quentin Copperfield appeared at his desk, just as he had thousands of times before. Seeing him on the news was one of Scarlet's first memories. "What is my daddy doing in that tiny box?" she'd thought.

"Good evening. My name is Quentin Copperfield. It's March 13th, 2023, and this is the nightly news."

"Whoop!" Ivy and James cheered. Greta joined them, clapping her hands.

Over the next thirty minutes, Quentin read the news with expert precision. He talked about evacuations, refugees, sporting events, and poverty, and he did it with authority in a way that guided the American people through the evening.

After he concluded with the news, Quentin cleared his throat.

"As many of our viewers know, this is my first night back at the station in quite some time. It is very good, if bittersweet, to be back. For seventeen years, I have sat in this chair and delivered the news in a way that I hope was respectful and honest. But I am sorry to report that my tenure at this station must come to an end."

All of the Copperfields remained very quiet.

"The past few months have called attention to what's truly important," he continued. "And I've decided to return to my childhood home on Nantucket to better my relationship with my children, wife, parents, siblings, nieces, and nephews. I was lucky enough to be born into a fantastic family— and it's high time I stop pretending we have infinite time to spend together. Life is fleeting. And I plan to spend as much of mine with the ones I love.

"So, for the very last time, this is Quentin Copperfield, wishing you a happy and healthy evening wherever you are. Thank you, and goodnight."

The news transitioned to a commercial for fitness-friendly cereal. At The Copperfield House, the family reeled.

"My goodness," Greta said finally, breaking through the silence.

Scarlet hurried over to her mother, who wept into her

hands. As Ivy and James hurried toward them, she wrapped her arms around Catherine. Together, the four of them held each other, their hearts full of expectations for the future. They couldn't wait for Quentin to return home.

# Chapter Twenty-One

The first day of spring was set for March 20th. Because Nantucketers find any reason to celebrate— and go all out for the said celebration, the Saturday directly before the big seasonal change was the official Nantucket Springtime Celebration.

James was the most excited of any of the Copperfields. This was because the annual spring celebration always began with a morning baseball scrimmage between Nantucket High School and Martha's Vineyard's Edgartown High School, which was located just across the Sound. At the breakfast table, Scarlet, Ivy, Catherine, and Greta watched as James scrambled around to prepare for the game. He adjusted his baseball hat over his ears three times, buttoned and unbuttoned his jersey, and poured himself a cup of coffee that Catherine ultimately made him throw out.

"You don't want to be jittery for your first game," she said.

Danny, a senior at Nantucket High, had also made the baseball team. He appeared in the kitchen bright-eyed and ready to go, seemingly not nervous at all. Together, he and

James grabbed pieces of toast and headed into the blue-skied morning to meet their team at the field. When the front door closed after them, everyone at the breakfast table breathed a sigh of relief.

"He was making me so nervous!" Ivy shook her head and sipped her coffee like a much older woman than eighteen.

"It's rare to see James so excited about something," Catherine said.

"I saw him walking around town the other day with a few boys," Scarlet said conspiratorially. "They grabbed sodas and headed to the boardwalk to watch the boats. It was so wholesome, like a Norman Rockwell painting."

"There they are!" Quentin walked into the kitchen in a pair of running shorts and a baseball hat. "Did I miss James?"

"He just left," Catherine explained as she stood slowly to kiss Quentin on the lips. "But we have to be at the baseball field at ten-thirty sharp."

"Not a problem," Quentin said. He placed two pieces of bread in the toaster and hummed to himself. Sweat from his beach run gleamed along his neck. "I saw Julia out there this morning. She looked faster than me, so I kept a wide berth. I don't want her to know how out of shape I am."

"What's that?" Alana stepped into the kitchen with a mischievous grin. "You wanted me to tell Julia something?"

Quentin's cheeks burned. "Don't you dare tell her. She'll find out on her own one of these days, anyway."

Alana flipped her hair over her shoulders. "I don't know why you two run on the beach, anyway. You're masochists. Jeremy does the same thing." Jeremy was Alana's current and previous boyfriend and also the captain of the football team. Scarlet really liked him— but more than that, she liked the way Jeremy always looked at Alana, as though she was a goddess, and he was just lucky to tag along.

Ivy and Scarlet went upstairs to get dressed and do their hair and makeup. As they lined their eyes with black eyeliner, Ivy spoke at length about the schedule she'd decided upon for her first semester at NYU. Scarlet still hadn't signed up for any classes, which both devastated and terrified her. Why was her little sister so clear about her goals, while Scarlet felt so scattered?

As Scarlet stuffed her makeup back into her cosmetics case, she heard herself say, "Maybe I'll extend my break from NYU."

Ivy hesitated. Her eyes were heavy with worry. "Are you close to having enough credits to graduate?"

Scarlet had just looked into it. In three and a half years, she'd changed her major so many times and collected credits from all corners of the university.

"Weirdly, I almost always took a history class," Scarlet told Ivy. "I never in my wildest dreams considered majoring in history."

"I remember you spent that semester in Rome. You must have had a lot of history classes, then," Ivy pointed out.

"Yes. I did always love them." Scarlet paused. "But where does a major in history even take you?"

Ivy shrugged. "Ask Dad?"

At the baseball game, Scarlet, Ivy, and Catherine sat under thick blankets and bundled themselves up in coats, scarves, hats, and mittens. The temperature was in the fifties, and the sun shone confidently above them, but sitting still for hours at a time was a first-class ticket to illness. None of the Copperfields had time for that.

Quentin was up ahead of them, leaning against the fence with a guy he'd introduced as "a friend from high school." It was funny to see her father with such ease about him, cracking jokes with a guy he'd known forever.

"I've never even seen your father like this," Catherine whispered conspiratorially.

Off to the right, the rest of the remaining Copperfields had gathered. Greta and Bernard spoke easily with old friends, probably ones they'd known for decades. Ella and Will chatted with other baseball parents as Alana, Jeremy, Julia, and Charlie ate popcorn and drank hot coffee. The rest of the cousins had returned home but sent frequent updates, urging James and Danny to "have a great game!" Their love was palpable, even across the continent.

Midway through the first inning, it was James's turn at bat. He walked out to home base with his shoulders back, and his chest puffed out. Only his immediate family members sensed the tension in his face; he was nervous.

Unfortunately for the Nantucket team, the Edgartown pitcher was top-rate. There were whispers of him getting a college scholarship to an Ivy League school. Scarlet didn't like those odds. Still, she cupped her mouth with her hands and cried, "Go get 'em, James!"

"I'm going to throw up," Ivy whispered.

The pitcher drew his arm and leg backward and then forward with insane inertia. The ball snapped into the catcher's mitt in no time flat.

"I didn't even see the ball," Scarlet admitted.

From the fence, Quentin turned to look at his family with dread. *Could James do this?*

"Come on, buddy," Catherine muttered.

Yet again, the pitcher shot the ball toward the catcher so quickly that James hardly flinched. Scarlet's stomach knotted up.

"This is his last chance," Ivy said.

And suddenly, the ball came toward James. This time, instead of standing there with a blank expression on his face, James took a risk and flung his bat forward. Miraculously, the bat hit the ball, and the ball went wild into the field directly behind third base. For a moment, James stood and watched the ball as it whipped across the blue sky.

"RUN, JAMES!" Quentin cried.

James finally remembered the rules of baseball. He stretched his long legs into a sprint toward first base. Although it wasn't necessary, he slid into it, as though he wanted to act out what he'd seen in baseball movies. The entire crowd cheered.

Scarlet, Ivy, and Catherine hugged each other excitedly as Quentin and Kenny high-fived. Around them, the crowd was quintessentially wholesome. Nobody cared that James was Quentin Copperfield's son. He was just James, their new ballplayer. Beyond that, he could be whoever he wanted to be. What a blessing that was.

By the time one-thirty hit, the scrimmage was complete at a tie. Both coaches spoke on the megaphone to thank everyone for coming out. "Don't you dare miss the annual Springtime Celebration downtown," the coach of Nantucket High warned. "Our Nantucket community has worked tirelessly to put up a festival to welcome the new warm-ish weather. They're telling me there's plenty of clam chowder, lobster rolls, sweet treats, and much more to go around. I know our baseball boys here have worked up quite the appetite. Let's give them all a round of applause, shall we?"

James and Danny said goodbye to their teammates and hurried over to the Copperfields for another round of hugs and high-fives. James's cheeks were blotchy with red, and his eyes danced as he narrated his first hit as though none of them had witnessed it firsthand. Scarlet beamed with pride.

Together, the family walked downtown to grab a bite to eat and engage in the festivities. The temperature had lifted into the low sixties, and Scarlet removed her hat and swung out her dark curls. Greta patted her shoulder kindly and said, "You're looking beautiful as ever, my darling."

Once downtown, Scarlet waited in line with her father to grab bowls of clam chowder for James, Ivy, and Catherine, who'd grabbed a picnic table near the bandstand. Later that afternoon, Ella and Will would perform their music for the island, and they'd returned home to grab their equipment. As Scarlet and Quentin waited, several Nantucketers approached to say hello and welcome Scarlet to the community. When asked what she was up to, Scarlet explained she was a student at NYU but had taken a semester break. Every time she had to say it, a rush of fear came over her, so much so that by the time they neared the front of the line, she swam with anxiety.

"Are you okay?" her father asked timidly.

Scarlet shifted her weight. "I thought I would know what I wanted by now. I dropped out of school like nine weeks ago for crying out loud."

"Nine weeks?" For a moment, Scarlet thought Quentin was going to get angry, but he just shook his head and smiled. "Nine weeks is nothing. You have to be patient with yourself."

The knots in Scarlet's stomach loosened. After another pause, she said, "I added up my credits and found out I'm really close to a history degree. But what can I do with a history degree?"

Quentin's eyes widened. "History? Gosh, Scarlet. I had no idea you were so interested in history!" Wildly, he waved toward his high school buddy, Kenny, until he approached. Scarlet swam in disbelief. When Kenny got there, Quentin said, "Kenny, you'll never believe what my daughter just told me. Tell him, Scarlet."

Scarlet stuttered. "Um. I told you I almost have a degree in history?"

Kenny's eyes widened, then he smiled. He clapped Quentin on the shoulder and cried, "We got another one!"

Quentin smiled with pride. "So, in these classes, you've

probably learned a lot about researching? About digging into the past? About categorizing the information you've found?"

"Yeah. Sure." Scarlet shrugged. "I was surprised how much I didn't hate it. Even the 'boring' parts." She used air quotes.

Kenny and Quentin exchanged excited glances.

"What is this about?" Scarlet demanded.

Conspiratorially, Quentin said, "When I decided to leave the news station, I spoke with Kenny about making history documentaries about Nantucket."

"We want to start with the whaling industry," Kenny explained. "I work at the Whaling Museum, so I have access to hundreds of archives."

"Would you be interested in helping us out?" Quentin asked. "Going through these archives is tedious, and we could really use someone with your historical expertise."

"Expertise? I wouldn't call it that," Scarlet began.

But Quentin interrupted her. "You have to learn to talk the talk," he explained. "Nobody is going to believe in what you're doing unless you believe in it, too."

"But what if I don't yet?" Scarlet asked.

"That's part of the game," Quentin explained. "Nobody knows what they're doing. Nobody knows anything."

"History is a great reminder of that," Kenny went on. "We have the privilege of future knowledge as we look back. But the deeper I get into the history of humans, the more I understand that we're always a little bit lost."

Scarlet couldn't help but smile.

"Just think about it," her father urged her. "It would be a great way to spend the summer."

Scarlet knew in her bones he was right.

# Chapter Twenty-Two

The doctor called Catherine back to the city at the beginning of April. For the first time in years, Quentin found himself at the wheel of their car, driving Catherine back to New York as the April sunlight glittered through the front window. Although they were both nervous, he and Catherine chatted gently about the growing springtime, the buds on the trees, and the way the Nantucket Sound looked especially turquoise when the light hit it just so.

Because Quentin's life was much more lowkey, he'd let go of his primary driver and his secondary driver, both of whom had picked up immediate work with other newscasters at the station. The primary driver had gone with the person who had taken Quentin's place, a woman named Amelia. She was the first solo female anchor in the history of broadcast television, and Quentin was terribly proud of his old station for making the jump. Both Ivy and Scarlet respected the move a great deal and begged to meet Amelia the next time they were in New York.

Once in the city again, Quentin parked the car in a parking

garage and hurried around to help Catherine from the front seat. She swatted him away and laughed.

"I'm not so weak anymore, Q. I can open and close a door myself."

Quentin and Catherine walked into the doctor's office with their chins held high. Whatever the news was, they would handle it together. They had to. They'd been put on this earth to be a team.

Catherine had had her blood drawn a week ago in Nantucket. The blood had been tested, and the results had been sent directly to Catherine's oncologist in the city. They would show whether or not Catherine's cancer had been defeated after months of chemo and her mastectomy. Regardless of the outcome, the news would alter the course of their lives forever.

To keep Catherine's mind off the matter of the test results, Quentin tried to joke with her in the waiting room. He imitated his father's singing voice, which Bernard shared with them every night as he played the piano. He joked about Alana's vanity, Julia's silliness, and Catherine's newfound obsession with walking the beach while listening to true crime podcasts. He spoke quickly, his smile crooked. His hope was that Catherine would crack a smile or a laugh. Often, she managed it.

When the doctor called them in, Quentin and Catherine sat, holding hands as they waited. The doctor clasped his own hands over the table and told them the test results were back—and that, for the time being, Catherine was in the clear.

"We will know if it's completely gone five years from now," he explained. "But it seems the chemo and surgery worked wonders. Congratulations. You did it."

Catherine's face crumpled. Silently, she pressed her face against Quentin's chest as he held her.

"Thank you, Doctor," Quentin said. "Thank you so much."

Too exhilarated to get back in the car, Quentin and Catherine walked many blocks back to their apartment in the Upper West Side. Frequently, Catherine paused to gaze up at buildings or admire street art. She did it with the fresh eyes of a woman who'd just been told she was allowed to live again. Quentin took one photo of her, in which she removed her hat and allowed her first tufts of hair to shine in the sun. He loved her so completely, and he told her so many times on their walk back home that she giggled and told him to cool it.

Back in the home where they'd raised their children, they made tea, sat at the window, and gazed out at the view that had been theirs for so many years. They recounted old memories, both good and bad, and agreed they didn't regret a single moment.

Around four-thirty, the doorbell rang, and Quentin asked the doorman to send them up. The elevator opened to a young couple in their late thirties who introduced themselves as Marvin and Claudia. Claudia's eyes bugged out as she scanned the first room and the attached kitchen.

"This place is extraordinary," she breathed.

"We think so," Catherine said, following behind Claudia as she walked through the kitchen and touched the countertops.

Over the next half-hour, Claudia and Marvin peppered Quentin and Catherine with questions about the apartment building, the amenities, the school district, and their favorite restaurants. By the time five hit, the look in their eyes told Catherine and Quentin they were prepared to take it.

"It's just a short-term lease for now," Quentin explained.

"We were thinking a year?" Catherine said. "But there is a possibility we won't want to come back."

Claudia's face beamed with hope they never would.

"We raised our family here," Quentin explained. "Heck, we've lived in this city together for twenty-two years."

"All of our children were born in New York," Catherine said. "And leaving is not easy."

"Our children will adore this place," Claudia said.

"What ages are they?" Quentin asked.

"Twelve, ten, and eight," Marvin answered proudly.

"Great ages," Quentin affirmed.

"Every age is a great age," Catherine said.

After Marvin and Claudia disappeared down the elevator, Quentin and Catherine hugged for a long time, overwhelmed at their decision to leave. Despite each wave of sorrow, they were steady in their knowledge that it was the right decision. They had to make space for what came next— and the apartment in the city was too big to remain empty. A new family needed to fill it, to make memories there like they had. It was time.

# Chapter Twenty-Three

News of Owen's arrest had spread like wildfire. Scarlet's city friends called her nonstop for weeks afterward to update her on what they'd heard, most of which was just gossip. The gossip itself ranged from the impossible to the strange— either making Scarlet laugh or wince or a bit of both. According to gossip, Owen had done this kind of scheming to at least four other women, that he was actually Russian and was being sent back to his country, and that Tiffany Bunny had been hypnotized into falling in love with him and now maintained she'd never seen that man in her life. Nobody knew what was real and what wasn't, and Owen wasn't exactly open with his facts. His lawyer had told him to keep his mouth shut before the trial. Then again, the facts of what he'd done to Scarlet had been captured on tape— and there wasn't a whole lot he could do to get out of it.

"But you're free," Alyssa said on the phone. "That guy is behind bars."

"Yes. But I can't help but beat myself up that I allowed him to manipulate me like that. Can I trust anyone ever again?"

"Around here, you can trust people," Alyssa explained. "I don't know anywhere better than Nantucket and Martha's Vineyard."

"Does that mean you're sticking around?" Scarlet wished Martha's Vineyard was connected to Nantucket by a bridge so that she and Alyssa could meet in the middle.

"I sort of have to stay on Martha's Vineyard now," Alyssa said with a laugh. "Things have certainly changed for me, but I'll tell you more details later."

"Intriguing," Scarlet said.

"I like to leave an air of mystery wherever I go," Alyssa joked.

It was the morning after Quentin and Catherine had called from the city to say Catherine was cancer free. As April winds cascaded across Nantucket beaches and made the big, old house creak, Scarlet hung up the phone and sat in the silence of herself. In front of her on the porch table sat piles and piles of historical records regarding the whaling boom that had more-or-less dictated Nantucket politics and economy for hundreds of years. Since she'd agreed to help her father and Kenny with their documentary, she'd allowed herself to fall back in love with history again, and she'd even signed up for a few online history courses through NYU. Maybe she didn't want to go back to the city after all. But that didn't mean she didn't want her degree.

Turns out, even though there had been plenty of twists and turns along the way, she'd always been working toward something. She just hadn't fully understood that yet.

A few hours later, the front door of The Copperfield House swung open to reveal Catherine and Quentin, fresh off their recent stint in the city. Catherine glowed with promise and health. As Ivy and James raced into her arms and called out that they loved them, Scarlet hung back and took in the splendor of the moment. Her father patted James on the shoulder as Ivy cried freely.

Down the hall, Alana, Julia, and Ella laughed about something as they set the table for an afternoon meal. The kitchen sizzled with Greta's cooking as Bernard creaked around in his study upstairs. Danny was somewhere, maybe with jock friends or running on the beach.

Here, the Copperfields were safe. They were together.

"Scarlet. Get over here." Her father beckoned playfully.

Scarlet raced toward her family and burrowed between Ivy and James. There in the warm embrace of her siblings, she closed her eyes. Together, they'd fought bravely through every coming storm. Now, they prepared themselves for the warmth of a new season, one of health, prosperity, and love, on the Island of Nantucket, their new home.

* * *

Coming Next in the Nantucket Sunset Series
Pre Order Nantucket in Bloom

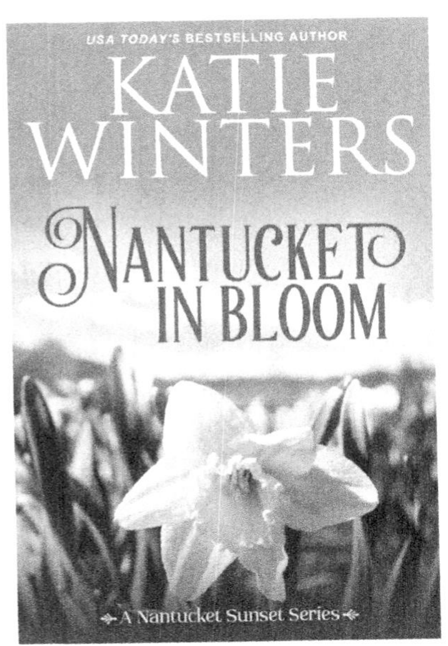
USA TODAY'S BESTSELLING AUTHOR
KATIE WINTERS
NANTUCKET IN BLOOM
A Nantucket Sunset Series

# Other Books by Katie

The Vineyard Sunset Series

A Nantucket Sunset Series

Secrets of Mackinac Island Series

Sisters of Edgartown Series

A Katama Bay Series

A Mount Desert Island Series

# Connect with Katie Winters

BookBub
Facebook
Newsletter